# The Complete TILLING

hat had been chosen in a similar dark blue to set off the overall effect. He was just admiring his reflection in a shop window when he spotted Elizabeth Mapp-Flint hurrying across the street.

"No time to stop," she called over. "So busy."

With that she disappeared into Diva Plaistow's house without stopping to knock.

"Must be important," Georgie thought, "to warrant such a hurry." She usually wanted to stop if only to find out what Lucia was up to.

Rounding the corner, he almost but bumped into Irene and her American friend. Georgie couldn't help but notice he was wearing a short double-breasted fawn coloured jacket. It had smart epaulets and looked slightly military. His trousers were of a check pattern and Georgie observed they were quite tight around his hips. Since the end of the war Georgie had noticed that fashion was changing and he liked to feel he was keeping up with the trends. Looking at the American, though, he suddenly felt outdated and wished he hadn't worn the rather ostentatious hat.

"I was just about to call on you," he said.

"Georgie, King of my heart, just the person. I've been dying to introduce you to my visitor, Colin. He's over from America and wants to meet all the spiffing artistic types that we have in the town. I, of course, immediately thought of you and Lucia."

"Well that's very kind," said Georgie. "I was hoping to invite you both to *Mallards* some time for supper. I must speak to Lucia first but I'm sure we can arrange something soon."

"How super!" said Irene "By the way, Colin is a 'friend of Dorothy' and as soon as he told me, you came to mind."

Throughout this exchange Colin hadn't spoken but upon the mention of Dorothy he stepped forward.

"So nice to meet you, Georgie," he said, taking his hand. "I'm sure we'll be great friends." Georgie was a little taken aback by his forwardness but assumed this was the way with Americans.

"Oh I'm sure we will," he replied with a smile, "but I don't know who you mean by Dorothy."

He couldn't for the life of him think of anyone called Dorothy. There was the assistant in the sweet shop they called Dodo but they couldn't mean her as she was always grumpy and could barely bother to pass the time of day when Georgie went in for his fruit drops. He had a vague memory of meeting someone called Dorothea once but couldn't recall where. Still the young man seemed very nice, was exceedingly handsome and still had hold of his hand.

"Don't be silly, Georgie," said Irene. "Of course you do, the Wizard of Oz girl."

Georgie was even more confused. He remembered trying to read the book when he was young but not finding it to his liking. "Not a patch on 'Alice in Wonderland'," he remembered thinking. Now if they had said a 'friend of Alice' that would have been much better. Still, he put it out of his mind and decided it was just one of Quaint Irene's silly notions.

"I would really like you to show me some of the best bits of the town as I hope to do some work while I'm here." Colin looked pleadingly at Georgie when he said this and Georgie was immediately captivated. He suddenly realised they were still holding hands and letting go he said, "it will be my pleasure."

At that moment Lucia appeared, looking a little flushed. She pulled herself together when she saw the trio on the corner and, putting two and two together, guessed that the young man clasping Georgie's hand a moment ago was the American artist she'd read about in the paper.

"Well this is a nice surprise, Irene," she said as though she rarely saw her, when in fact she met her almost every day. "Who's your new friend? Not keeping him to yourself I hope?" She gave Colin her best smile.

Irene laughed, caught hold of Lucia by the hand and pulled her forward "Of course not, dear one, this is Colin from America, he's going to be staying with me for a while."

"Not your sort of companion, Irene." Lucia said winking at her.

"No, but you have to admit he is very nice to look at."

Colin began to look a little uncomfortable at this point and Georgie felt rather sorry for him. "Why don't I show you a little of the town now, Colin, and then you and Irene can come back for lunch. What do you think, Lucia?"

"Good idea, Georgie. I'll just finish my shopping and meet you all at *Mallards* in an hour."

With that she disappeared into the nearby florist's. Irene said she had to hurry off and make some phone calls about her up-coming visit to London so Georgie and Colin were left alone.

The morning was pure heaven for Georgie as he showed an appreciative Colin the highlights of the town and they decided on a spot to meet the next day to do some sketching. Lunch at *Mallards* was a happy occasion and Lucia made a note to involve Colin in her plans for the tableaux at the September fête.

2

August was a boring month for Georgie. He'd enjoyed the first week as he and Colin had been able to sketch together. In fact Georgie had been rather pleased and surprised by the results, particularly following one meeting he'd had with him. They had decided on a site at the top of the town with a fine view over the countryside. Georgie at first felt it would offer little to draw but Colin insisted it was ideal as a back-drop. Georgie hadn't noticed his turn of phrase at first and began to look round for a nice place to set up his equipment. He had almost decided on a corner where he could see the edge of the town as well as the fields below and the hills in the far distance when Colin called him and asked him to move to a different place with his back to the view.

"I'm not sure this is ideal," Georgie said. "I need a bit more going on in the picture if I'm to win the competition in September."

"Don't worry, you won't be doing much work. I have a plan you may like. Would you mind if I drew you with the view behind as background? I don't think I mentioned before that I'm really a portrait rather than a landscape artist and you would be an ideal subject, if you are agreeable." Georgie was speechless. He fiddled with his scarf and took his hat off and put it on again. "Well I'm very flattered, I don't know what to say."

This was the first time Georgie could remember not having a response to a situation. In fact, he was famous for his repartee, or so he thought. He couldn't believe that Colin wanted to draw him but he did feel he would make a good subject and even began to decide, to himself, the best pose to take.

"Don't say anything, I have it all worked out and you can see the end result before anyone else. If you don't like it I will destroy it. Now we need to get on or I won't get finished by the time of the competition."

Georgie spent the next few days sitting quietly being sketched. This was a new experience for him as he was used to chattering quite a lot, but each time he tried to speak, Colin asked him to keep still so that he could get Georgie's features just right.

Since then, the boredom had set in. Colin and Irene had gone to London for two weeks, Mr and Mrs Wyse were, as usual, in their house in Tuscany or somewhere like that, Diva Plaistow had gone to Riseholme to visit her friend Daisy Quantock and Lucia was so absorbed in creating her tableaux for the fête that he hardly saw her. It was clear, however, that something had happened as she had been all talk about holding the event at *Mallards*, but following a visit from Susan the previous week, the subject had been dropped. When questioned, she denied that she had said such a thing and all she was doing (in her small way) were the tableaux and that was quite enough. When Georgie had seen Elizabeth in the town, she had made a point of asking how 'dear Lucia' was as she hadn't seen her recently. Georgie knew that Elizabeth was trying to probe so he told her that Lucia was fine and 'very busy' with the entertainment for the fête.

In the last week of August Georgie and Colin resumed their sketching together. Georgie was now able to concentrate on his work as Colin had finished using him as a model and was completing the portrait at Irene's house. They worked together on Georgie's sketches with Colin giving advice and encouragement.

Georgie was right about Lucia. She'd received a visit from Susan Wyse a week ago. Lucia saw the Royce draw up outside as she sat in her favourite place by the window. Grosvenor showed Susan in.

"Susan, what a nice surprise!" She said as she rose to greet her. In fact, it was far from a nice surprise as she'd heard the Padre start to mention Mrs Wyse when she visited him, so she guessed something had already been arranged. She had also seen Diva Plaistow in the town the following day who told her that Elizabeth had been to see her with the news that Mrs Wyse was furious at Lucia's interference and she would be calling to 'sort it out once and for all'.

"Lucia. I felt I had to call as there has been some misunderstanding on your part. You must not have been aware that I had already agreed with the Padre to hold the late summer fête in the grounds of my house as I have a large field at the back at my disposal in which we plan to house a coconut shy and a roundabout for the children, I'm sure you will agree that within your delightful garden such things would not be possible without spoiling your lovely flowers and shrubs."

Lucia was stumped as it was true that there was little room for such plans. "My dear Susan, how naughty of me to spoil the plans you have made. I had no idea they had gone so far. I was merely following up a conversation I had with the Padre some time ago, which must have slipped his mind, about *Mallards* being the venue for the event."

This, of course, was completely untrue. She realised that her plan was not now going to work so thought the best thing would be to back down graciously.

"I will, of course, still plan the entertainment if that is all right with you, dear Susan."

"Yes, of course. I'm sure it will be wonderful given your reputation in that area."

In fact Mrs Wyse had begun to plan something herself but thought perhaps it would be too much to deny Lucia this aspect of the event and she could still include her plans in the timetable with or without Lucia's permission.

"I'm glad we have been able to sort things out so amicably, I didn't want to go on holiday without things being remedied, it would have spoilt my rest and be unfair to you as well. Well I must hurry off now as we have so much to do before going away. Mr Wyse sends his regards, by the way." Lucia called Grosvenor to show Mrs Wyse out. She watched as she was driven away in her Royce.

\*\*\*

Lucia had been busy all week with the preparations for the tableaux. She had already decided that Major Benjy should be Churchill and Georgie and Elizabeth, George VI and Queen Elizabeth in one of the tableaux. She knew that Diva would want to be involved so she thought that she would organize a 'Rule Britannia' tableau with herself as Britannia. Diva could be one of the adoring followers with Evie Bartlett. She envisaged a parade of sorts with people throwing flowers as she passed with her entourage. "I'm sure," she thought, "The Argus would want a picture of such a wonderful sight."

Just as she was sketching out her costume Georgie arrived back from his painting with Colin. As he entered the room she noticed that he didn't have his sketch pad with him.

"Do show me your work, Georgie dear," she said. "I've hardly seen you all week as you've been away with that Calum!"

"Not Calum, Lucia, Colin. Yes, I've had a lovely time but I think I'll keep my sketches hidden until they're finished and then you can help me decide which to put into the competition."

"I don't know, Georgino, you spend more time with that Colin than you do with me. I hope you're not getting too friendly as he goes back to America in October you know."

"You don't need to worry about me, Lucia. I would have thought you had enough to do with your tableaux."

Lucia thought that Georgie was a little sharp but didn't say anything. She resolved to speak to Irene about his relationship with Colin as soon as she had a moment. Georgie turned to leave.

"We must get ready, you know. We've been invited to Irene's for a musical evening. Colin apparently plays the guitar beautifully."

"Is there no end to his talents?" Lucia replied. "I shall look forward to hearing him."

Lucia had to admit that Colin played the guitar beautifully but she was still concerned that Georgie was getting too involved. She watched Georgie during the evening and saw that he didn't take his eyes off Colin. When she had a quick word with Irene all she said was, "well what do you expect? They're both 'friends of Dorothy', they're sure to get on."

Lucia wracked her brains to think who they knew called Dorothy. "Such a horrid name," she thought. There was that Dodo woman in the sweet shop but she rejected her as she knew that Georgie couldn't stand her. "And Dorothea Cortese, but we haven't kept in touch at all with her." She resolved to ask Georgie later when they were on their own. In the meantime, she decided she really must get on with her preparations for the fête which was now only a week away.

\*\*\*

As August came to an end, Georgie had completed about six sketches, four of which he had started to tint with his water paints. Colin had decided that they were all very good and that they would leave it up to Lucia to decide which one he should submit to the competition. Georgie and Colin were often seen about the town either in deep conversation or day-dreaming, very often arm in arm. It was on one of these occasions that Elizabeth and Diva bumped into them one morning in late August. Afterwards Georgie thought it rather odd as they were in a part of the town rarely visited by the two ladies but they appeared hurrying up behind them out of breath.

"What a surprise!" exclaimed Elizabeth. "So nice to see you Georgie. You are a bad boy. We've seen you both about for some time and you have yet to introduce us to your friend."

"Good morning, Elizabeth. Good morning, Diva. May I introduce Colin Summer, an American artist?"

"How delightful. If I didn't know better, I would have thought you were avoiding us Georgie. My dear Mr Summer, you must come to one of my gatherings. I'll send an invitation to Quaint Irene's."

"Thank you, but I won't be in Tilling much longer after the art competition. I must return to America to resume teaching at the university, the term will be starting soon."

"What a shame, we so looked forward to getting to know you a little better," said Diva. "Well perhaps next time you visit us you will stay longer. I'm sure Georgie would like that, wouldn't you Georgie?"

"Err, yes, yes very much," Georgie stuttered.

"I hear you will be judging the competition. I hope you will have a look at my little contribution. It's not very much but perhaps you will see some promise in it," said Elizabeth with what she thought was one of her winning smiles. "Well, we must be off. So much to do. I do hope we see you at the fête next week. Au reservoir." With that the two ladies hurried away.

"What a fuss they make," said Georgie as he caught hold of Colin's arm again. "Let's go to Diva's tearoom while she's out".

3

The day of the annual fête had arrived and Lucia was busy hauling costumes around with the help of Cadman. A small tent had been pitched in the corner of the field behind Mr and Mrs Wyse's house and this was to be used as a changing room and storage facility. A large roundabout and a coconut shy were situated in the middle of the field and a stage had been set up near the house for the various tableaux. Lucia had already run through the tableaux with the participants.

A problem had arisen with the Mapp-Flints: Elizabeth refused to let Georgie be George the sixth. As she was to be Queen Elizabeth, she wanted Benjy to be the King. As a result, Lucia had to rush round and try to find another Churchill. She considered it most inconvenient to have to sort it out at the last minute. "In any case," she thought, "Major Benjy looked nothing like George VI and Georgie certainly couldn't carry off the Churchill role."

In the end Mr Wyse kindly agreed to do it and Georgie was to be Hitler. He wasn't happy with the change and refused to wear the 'silly moustache', but Lucia eventually managed to win him round.

The second tableau was to be a display of the various sporting activities in the town and each of the town sports clubs were to send two people to show off their skills (without moving, of course, she'd emphasised).

The final tableau was the pièce-de-résistance. Lucia would be dressed all in white as Britannia and they would play 'Rule Britannia' on the gramophone while she did a tour of the crowd with an entourage made up principally of Diva and Evie. So, despite the initial problem with Elizabeth, all was ready. Lucia was busy sorting the costumes in the tent when Susan Wyse appeared carrying a large suitcase.

"I'll just pop this here for later," she said.

"Of course, darling Susan." Lucia was trying to be especially nice to her following the recent misunderstanding. "What's in it?"

"Oh, nothing much, just a costume I thought I'd wear later if that's all right."

Lucia wasn't really listening as she'd notice a stain on her white Britannia costume and was busy trying to rub it off with her handkerchief. At this point, Georgie appeared with Colin and Irene.

"Come quickly, Lucia." said Georgie. "Elizabeth's making a fuss as usual about the art competition. She wants the Mayor to make sure her painting is near the door so it can be seen. Said the hall's too dark to do it justice. The Mayor told her, they had already decided where each painting was to go and that was that".

"I don't know what I can do, they'll have to sort it out between them. I'm much too busy here."

The tableaux were to start at 4 o'clock and Lucia had supervised the setting up of the first display. Elizabeth appeared in a furious mood and said she would bring the Mayor's conduct to the attention of the council at the next meeting. Lucia tried to say the right thing as she didn't want to rub Elizabeth up the wrong way, so while she helped her into her costume, a smart suit and large hat to match, she said how unfair the Mayor had been and she was sure it would be resolved tomorrow.

Major Benjy and Mr Wyse and been ready for some time. Mr Wyse was enjoying the cigar Lucia had given him and she was now worried that he would have smoked it before the tableau started. Georgie returned and donned the German uniform but still insisted he would not stick the moustache on. In the end Lucia persuaded him to put up with a black mark made with her eyebrow pencil.

When the curtains opened, everyone gasped with delight. Mr Wyse looked exactly like Churchill, but poor Georgie, who had to lie on the floor with Churchill's foot on him, felt humiliated. He cheered up later when someone told him that the whole thing looked very realistic.

The second tableau turned into a farce as none of the sports players would stand still, they all wanted to show off their skills. Major Benjy insisted on swinging his golf club dangerously. The cricketers started to bowl a ball and the batsman gave it a hefty swipe, nearly knocking the tennis ladies off the stage. Even the footballers felt the need to show off their skills and started to dribble their ball round the stage. In the end the two nine pin bowling men became angry when people kept knocking their pins over and left the stage in a huff. Lucia decided that she needed to call a halt to the proceedings and brought the curtain down. To her surprise there was much applause and laughter.

Finally, it was Lucia's moment. She had arranged for Diva and Evie to get ready and be on stage while she dressed. When she entered the tent, she was almost knocked aside by Susan Wyse coming out. She was dressed in a shiny silver dress with a sceptre in one hand and a union jack shield in the other. Without a word she jumped onto the stage, the curtains opened and 'Rule Britannia' blared out from the loud speaker. The two ladies, there to support Lucia, although surprised, played their part as instructed.

"You're supposed to parade round the crowd," whispered Diva.

With that Mrs Wyse stepped down from the stage and walked sedately around the audience. Everyone clapped and cheered while Lucia stood

rooted to the spot trying to look pleased although silently, she was furious. At the end of the show, Lucia took a quick bow on stage as the 'production manager' and left the fête to return home feeling dejected.
***
When Georgie got home, Lucia had begun to get over the disappointment. "Did you see what happened, Georgie?" she asked.

"I saw Susan Wyse as Britannia, a role I thought you'd decided to play. Did she know you were doing it and copied you on purpose do you think?"

"I don't know, Georgie. Apart from you the only other people who knew were Diva and the Evie. It looked to me as though they were as surprised as I was when Susan jumped on stage."

"We may never know, but don't feel too bad, people really enjoyed the tableaux and they know that you organised them. Go to bed and let's hope that the art competition has a better outcome."

"I've had no time to paint anything this year," she said, "but I'm hoping that lovely painting I chose of yours does well."

She gave Georgie a quick peck and went upstairs. Georgie could tell that she was upset and decided to stay close to her tomorrow at the competition.


4

Lucia and Georgie arrived at the Town Hall together the next morning. After the fête, yesterday Colin had taken Georgie to see his portrait which was still at Irene's house.

"Georgie, you must say if you don't like it and I will refuse to let them show it tomorrow."

"I'm sure it will be fine," said Georgie who was quite excited at the prospect of seeing it now it was finished. Colin had propped it against the dining table with a cloth over it. He asked Georgie to stand a little back against the wall as he removed the cloth. Georgie could hardly believe his eyes. It was beautiful. He was portrayed sitting on the town wall with the fields and hills as a backdrop. He was wearing his dark blue jacket and matching hat, but the surprise was his face. True, he looked younger, but it was his expression that was striking: he was staring straight ahead as though looking at someone in front of him and he had a slight smile.

"Not really in character," Georgie thought. But it was just right and reflected how he felt at the time of the sittings. He could hardly speak and he felt tears coming to his eyes.

"It's wonderful," he said, "but much too flattering. People will never believe it's me."

"It's how I see you," said Colin "and that's all that matters."

***

As Georgie and Lucia entered the hall Georgie could see Colin with Irene standing next to his painting, which was covered with a cloth in the middle of the room.

"I'm looking forward to seeing your picture," said Lucia as they walked over. "Irene, have you seen it yet?"

"Not fully completed, but I did see some early sketches and it looked super."

At that moment, the townspeople began to arrive. Most prominent were the Wyses followed by the Mapp-Flints and Diva Plaistow. The Mayor came over and asked Colin if he would start judging the pictures which had been hung round the walls. Quaint Irene's picture was among the first he looked at. It seemed to be of two women intertwined but the angles were very sharp and the colours bright.

Colin looked at each picture carefully, Diva's was a nice view of the church and a little further on Mr Wyse had painted some ships on the estuary. Mrs Wyse's was of some flowers in her garden, all quite accomplished and Colin felt he had a difficult job to decide on the winner. Next came Elizabeth's effort, a rather understated view from her house. As she lived in a rather flat area just outside the town it was rather unimpressive. Colin hardly glanced at it. Lucia looked across at Elizabeth when this happened and could see that she was less than happy. Colin spent some time looking at Georgie's and the Mayor's pictures, the latter being just a drawing of his Mayoral chain. Finally, in the corner was the picture by Evie Bartlett. It was quite small but a good likeness of the Padre.

"Well," said Colin to the crowd, "I've been very impressed by the standard today and it has been a very difficult decision. In third place I must put George Pillson's view of the town, it shows a good eye for perspective and the colour wash sets it off well."

Georgie smiled round and flapped his handkerchief with embarrassment.

"Second is Mr Wyse. A very well-constructed painting of the ships which gives a clear idea of movement. But first prize must go to Mrs Bartlett who has caught the Padre's likeness exactly. Well done!"

There was polite applause as Evie, with a squeak, stepped forward to collect her trophy from the Mayor.

At this point Lucia noticed Elizabeth hurrying out with Major Benjy in tow. She was just heard to say, "Rubbish" as she went out the door.

"Now," said the Mayor "we must unveil Mr Summer's painting which he has kindly donated to the town and it will have pride of place in the Town Hall."

As he pulled the cloth from the picture, there was a slight gasp from the audience and Lucia said, "Wonderful!" and gave Georgie a hug. "He's done a marvellous job."

\*\*\*

When Georgie came down to breakfast the next day he found Lucia at the table looking at the local newspaper. She was smiling to herself.

"Look, Georgie, you're on the front page."

Georgie took the paper from her and was surprised to see a half-page picture of Colin's portrait with the caption 'World renowned artist's painting of local character to take pride of place in the Town Hall'.

"How wonderful!" said Georgie. "I'm so pleased. But… what do they mean by 'character'?"

"Oh, that's just the way they write. It means you're popular."

"Does it really? I never knew I was. I hope Colin's seen it. I'm due to call this morning, he said it was most important. I don't know what it could be."

"Wait Georgie, you haven't seen the best part."

She turned to the second page which contained the headline 'Mrs Lucia Pillson's tableaux were the highlight of the autumn fête'. No mention of Mrs Wyse, just a description of the three tableaux.

"It's about time the Argus acknowledged the work I do in the town. Susan Wyse has been getting all the coverage lately. I must make sure she's seen this."

Foljambe appeared with Georgie's egg at that moment and Georgie sat down to eat it.

"Colin is going back to America soon. He must be there for the start of the academic year he says, although I not quite sure what that means. I expect he'll explain when I see him later."

"Now, Georgie, you mustn't get yourself too upset. I'm sure he'll come back again another year and we will have so much to do preparing for harvest festival, not to mention Christmas."

"Oh I suppose so," he said, finishing his egg. He quickly drank his tea. "I must hurry off. I said I'd be round at Irene's by ten."

As Georgie left *Mallards* a figure was seen peeping round the corner at the end of the street. Mrs Elizabeth-Flint appeared as soon as he was gone and hurried up to the front door. Grosvenor answered her knock and ushered her into the garden room where Lucia was at the piano. Lucia had been sorting out some pieces of music that she could play with Georgie at their next cultural evening get-together.

"Dear Lucia, always so musical," Elizabeth said. "I was just passing and thought I'd pop in to congratulate you on your wonderful tableaux at the fête, so delightful. I saw the Argus today and thought I should come round at once."

The truth was that Elizabeth's reason for 'popping round' had nothing to do with the Argus. She had been in town last evening on her way to see Diva when she bumped into Irene and Colin coming out of Mr Twistevant's shop.

"Going to celebrate the success of the art competition, I suppose," she said in an unfriendly manner.

"Now Mapp, don't be a bad loser. You have to admit most of the paintings were better than your effort," replied Irene

"I'm not a bad loser. I'm pleased that the Padre's wife won first prize. I was surprised that Georgie's washed out effort came third, though. Still, I have notice you are very close." She looked directly at Colin as she spoke. "It won't be long, so I hear, before you go back to America. Such a sad loss to Georgie and you, Irene."

"Not such a sad loss," snapped Irene. "As it happens I will be going back for a while with Colin to help with his art class at the University and we intend to ask Georgie to join us." Irene suddenly stopped and looked at Colin. "Sorry, we said we wouldn't tell anyone until we'd asked him. You must promise not to breathe a word, Mapp."

"Dear Irene, of course not if you say so. I'm just off to Diva's and will be discretion itself."

Irene looked a little worried at this as she moved off with Colin. Calling a hasty "Goodnight." Elizabeth almost ran to Diva's house in her excitement at the news.

At *Mallards*, Elizabeth settled herself in Lucia's garden room. "Georgie not at home?"

"No, you just missed him he's on his way round to see Irene. Something important, he said."

"He's become very close to Irene recently. Usually they don't see eye to eye on everything but I expect it's Colin he really goes to see. So close, so nice to see him making such a good friend." At this point she decided to drop the bombshell she had really come round to deliver. "You will so miss him when he goes."

"Goes? Goes where?"

"Why, to America. Has he not told you he's been invited to join Irene and go to America to help Colin with his Art Class at the university?"

Lucia was stunned. She was silent for a moment but with an effort managed to pull herself together.

"Oh yes! Yes, that. Of course, I'll miss him but I won't stand in his way. It's a great opportunity for him."

"Yes, dear Lucia, so brave. Now you mustn't be on your own at Christmas. You are always welcome at *Grebe*, as you know." She said this without much conviction. "Now I must away, so much to do. I'll see myself out. Au Reservoir."

The deed done, she disappeared out the door. Lucia sat quietly for a moment looking at the sheet music she had planned to use and with a sigh she swept it to the floor.

\*\*\*

Meanwhile Georgie had arrived at Irene's and was met by Colin.

"No Irene?" he said

"No, she just stepped out. Georgie, I have something important to ask you. As you know I will be returning to America next week and Irene has agreed to come back with me for a few months. I wondered if you would also like to come. Please take some time to think about it. I know it's a big decision to make."

Georgie was speechless for a few moments.

"To America… how wonderful! Well I do need time to think about it and I will need to consult Lucia of course." He stood up and took a deep breath. "Thank you, Colin, for asking me. I have enjoyed our outings together and feel we have become good friends. Indeed, friends of Dorothy, as you say, although I still can't recall her. I will discuss this with Lucia today and let you know in the morning."

\*\*\*

So that was it, the 'big decision' he had to make. In truth, he felt he wanted to go, but on the other hand he didn't want to leave Lucia. He walked slowly back home hoping to catch Lucia before she went out. On his way, he saw Elizabeth lurking at the end of the road but pretended not to see her. The last thing he needed was such a meeting. She would be sure to see something was troubling him and he could do without her advice on the matter.

When he entered the garden room he found Lucia on her hands and knees picking up sheet music. "All slipped to the floor," she said. "Such a nuisance."

Georgie looked at her scrabbling about under the piano. He could see she was upset about something. "Let me give you a hand," he said and got down on his hands and knees and they both collected up the bits of paper, banging their heads on the piano and laughing at their incompetence.

Once collected up, Lucia sat at the piano and sorted the sheets into order. "A little set of tunes I thought we could play together sometime."

Georgie watched her quietly and began to realise he couldn't go to America with Colin however much he wanted to. He loved it at *Mallards* with Lucia, their musical evenings playing the piano together, or sometimes she would play while he did his embroidery. He couldn't envisage feeling happy so far away in America, even with Colin present, who would be busy with his University work. And as for Irene, there was no saying what she would be up to. No, he would stay here at home where he was happy and where he felt loved.

"Colin has asked me to go to America with him and Irene."

"Oh really? That sounds grand."

"Yes, but I've decided not to go."

"What. Why? Georgie, it's a wonderful opportunity for you to see the world."

"I don't want to see the world, Lucia. I want to stay here with you."

"Oh Georgie, I don't know what to say."

"Nothing," he said. "There is nothing more to say. I will get ready for lunch."

He got up from the chair walked over and gave Lucia a peck on the cheek.

As he made his way slowly upstairs, there was a slight tear in his eye and he paused to look round. "Well, life is strange," he said to himself. As he continued up the stairs he began to think about Colin and what great friends they'd been.

"He was right, I am a friend of Dorothy, and what's more, I always will be."


The End

## Daisy Quantock on the Move

## 1

Daisy Quantock was in the mood for a change, she'd been thinking recently about the two friends she'd lost. Lucia had moved from Riseholme and although they hadn't always seen eye to eye, they had been involved in several local events which now lacked Lucia's flare. Georgie had moved with her further depleting Daisy's group of friends. She was beginning to think that Riseholme was not what it used to be, no Literary Society to speak of and the May Day fair was reduced to a few stalls and a bit of a dance round the Maypole, in fact last year it had rained so much the whole event had to be cancelled. She had visited Lucia in Tilling a few times over the years and made friends with some of the other Tillingites so she had now come to a decision.

"Robert, put the paper down and listen to me for a change, I've decided that we are not getting any younger and should decide what we want to do with the rest of our lives."

"Do we? Yes I suppose we do, aren't you happy with what we do now?"

"No I'm not, everything we do seems to be a disaster, the Riseholme Museum fire, the May Day pageant wash out, not to mention the Golf Club incident, I've had enough of it!"

"Daisy don't be silly that was years ago. You've tried loads of things since then, Christian Science, yoga, spiritualism why not do some of those again or move on and get involved in something new."

"No, I've decided we need to move to a new house and I want go to Tilling."

"What, Tilling! Why you're always at odds with Lucia and you can't stand that Mapp woman, why Tilling?"

"I just feel there is more going on there, they have a summer fete, an art exhibition, a super golf course and what's more it's nearer the sea. We should look at the house prices and think about moving."

"Well if you really want to, go over and visit Lucia and your friend Diva whatever her name is."

\*\*\*

Elizabeth Mapp-Flint had also made her mind up. She had been awake all night thinking things over, listening to the rain on the bedroom window and had come to a decision. She was tired of the continual worry about flooding, she still remembered when she had been swept out to sea on a table with Lucia and she feared something like it could happen again every time it rained.

Breakfast in the Mapp-Flint household was a formal affair, Elizabeth would read the local paper while her husband Major Benjy would look at the Telegraph financial pages. They each had porridge followed by toast and marmalade.

"Shares are down again, I don't know what's happening to the markets at the moment, they haven't recovered from the effects of the war, we are in a bad way old girl."

"Never mind about that Benjy, I've come to a decision, I think we should move house. I'm fed up with this damp place away from the town and likely to flood every winter."

"Um, are you? I suppose your right but I'm not sure we can afford to move, we have little savings and the markets are in the doldrums, our Siriami shares were never very good at the best of times but things are getting worse."

"That's just the point, Benjy, we could sell this place, buy a smaller town house and have money left over."

"If you say so old girl, but I'm not too worried as this weather nothing like the Jumna in flood. Still I'm happy to move if you want to, perhaps nearer the golf course."

"Benjy, that's no good the houses are too expensive there, I'll go into town this morning and have a look in the Estate Agents, Woolgar and Pipstow."

***

It was early February and the weather had been wet for a few days. Lucia was finding life a little dull, she always hated this time of the year after the excitement of Christmas and still two months until Easter. However, she hoped that things were looking up, the Mayor had stopped her on the high street a few days earlier and asked if she would consider organising an Easter Parade. He'd spoken to Reverend Bartlett, he said, and he'd also agreed that it would be a nice idea. They'd decided to plan a route from the town hall to the church and wanted Lucia to organise things as she'd done a good job in the past with similar events.

"They have one in Battersea Park in London you know," the Mayor informed her "and while ours would be on a smaller scale I'm sure we could get people interested."

Lucia was pleased to arrange everything as it would give her something to do over the winter. At that moment, she heard Georgie coming down the stairs.

"Is that 'oo, Georgino mio?" She called "come here and sit down I've something to discuss with you." He hurried into the room and settled in his favourite chair.

"When I was in London I went to the Easter Parade in Battersea Park, Georgie."

He was a little tired of hearing about Lucia's London exploits but tried to look interested. "Well the Mayor has asked me to organise one in Tilling."

"Really!" Said Georgie perking up "how exciting, what happens do we have to actually parade or something, I wonder what I should wear."

"It's not about you Georgie it's about the ladies' hats, a bit like Ascot. We'll parade round, or walk really, from the town hall to the church for an Easter service."

"Oh, still I shall have to decide what to wear, you'll need an escort surely."

Lucia was about to expand on her ideas when there was a knock on the door and Cadman came in with his wife Foljambe.

"Sorry to bother you," said Cadman "but I wondered if you had a moment."

"Yes, Cadman what is it, nothing too worrying I hope?"

"Well it's quite important really, you see Mrs Cadman and I feel we would like a change, I like my job driving and looking after your car but feel I need to strike out on my own, so I've decided to set up a driving school business. Everyone will have a car soon, according to the papers sales are going up all the time and people will need to learn to drive so I think it would be a good idea."

"This is a shock Cadman, you've been with me for over twenty years now, do you think you're ready for such a change at your age?"

"I'm only fifty and Mrs Cadman is younger than me so I think we could make a go of it."

"Foljambe what do you say?" asked Georgie who was looking more and more worried as Cadman spoke.

"Well Mr Georgie, I will be very sorry to leave you but I must support my husband's plans. We wouldn't need to go at once as it will take a while to arrange things so you'll have time to adjust you know."

"Oh dear," said Georgie "I don't know what I shall do without you, who will keep an eye on my bibelots and make sure all my things are in order. I don't know what I to say. Oh dear, Oh dear. I can't believe that everyone will have a car, horrid noisy things, I think you're both making a big mistake." With that he hurried from the room clearly very distressed.

"Well Cadman thank you for letting us know, I do realise that chauffeurs and maids are becoming a thing of the past and we must move with the times in this new age of socialism. We will just have to manage, Georgie will get over his shock eventually."

"I did feel, Mrs Pillson that I could still be of assistance. I thought I would ask you to be my first pupil and I would teach you, free of charge of course, that's if you would like to learn."

Lucia was a little startled by this she had never considered such a thing. Quaint Irene had been seen driving a car and she was sure that Mr Wyse could drive despite his use of the chauffeur, but she'd never considered doing it herself. The more she thought about it the more she liked the idea. She would be able to get about whenever she wanted and think of the surprise and envy of everyone when she drove through the town.

"Yes Cadman I think I should like that very much, when can we start?"

2

Luckily the rain had stopped when Elizabeth arrived in the town and she went straight to the estate agents to see what was available. She looked in the window and spotted there were quite a few nice houses near the golf course but, to her disappointment, they were out of her price range. There were also some smaller terraced properties near the station, most unsuitable she felt. Still she went in to the office and asked them to value her house as soon as possible. As she emerged she bumped into Diva doing her daily rounds of the shops. Diva was bundled up in a thick coat and rain hat which made her look bigger than ever.

"Buying a house Elizabeth?" She asked

"Don't tell anyone but we are thinking of moving. I do so love *Grebe* but Benjy Boy is not getting any younger and we really need to be in the town. Unfortunately, I've looked at what's on offer but can't find anything suitable either too small for us or too big, nothing just right."

"You mean nothing in your price range."

"We don't really know yet, Diva we are waiting to see what we can get for *Grebe*."

"Not much it's a damp hole."

"Well really if you can't be pleasant I'll leave you and get on." She snapped

"Sorry Elizabeth I'm having a bad morning, it's this dreadful weather. Listen, I've got an idea, why don't you look at old Mrs Ames's house next door to *Mallards*, she died last year and I know it's empty. She rather neglected it from all accounts so you might get it cheap if you don't mind the extra work."

Elizabeth knew the house not large but a nice old building. She didn't really know Mrs Ames, in her nineties never went out and quite infirm for some years, she remembered. She did hear that she'd been a firebrand in her day and died about a year ago. She resolved to go and have a look at the house straight away.

"Thank you, Diva dear I'll think about it but must get on so much to do. Au Reservoir."


The house stood directly on the road and Elizabeth tried peering in at the windows without much success. It was certainly empty and the rooms were a nice size but she felt she needed to have a better look round. There was a gate at the side and after glancing up the street she slipped through into the garden.
***

After Cadman left Lucia went up to Georgie's room and knocked but apart from some muffled sounds there was no reply. She thought it better to leave him until he'd recovered a little, so she returned to the garden room to relax. She decided to sit at the piano and play for a little while. The rain had stopped and a watery sun was showing through which cheered her up. She thought it wouldn't be so bad without Cadman once she could drive and after all there was still Grosvenor and Cook to look after her and Georgie. He really was making too much of a fuss but she knew how much he relied on Foljambe so she resolved to take more care of him in future. She opened the window a few inches to let in a little air and had just settled down at the piano when she heard someone shout.

"Cooee Lucia."

At first, she couldn't think where it was coming from but soon realised that there was someone outside. Standing up she looked out and was horrified to see Elizabeth looking over next door's wall. It was clear that she could see right into Lucia's room.

"About to play something, how pleasant. I will so enjoy hearing your music when we move in. It will be so nice to be close to *Mallards* again."

Lucia was shocked and opening the window wider she leant out, "what are you doing there Elizabeth, how did you get into next door's garden?"

"Just looking round. We intend to move and this house is ideal for me and Benjy boy. It will be lovely to be living back in the centre of the town right next door to you, dear Lucia. I'll be able to pop in so much more often." With that she bobbed down again behind the wall.

Lucia couldn't believe her eyes. She did know the house was empty and remembered Mrs Ames dying last year. She hadn't got to know her very well as she had been ill when Lucia moved to *Mallards*. She resolved to go to the estate agent at once and find out the price and the name of the seller. She was determined to stop Elizabeth moving next door at all cost.

When Lucia arrived at the estate agent to her surprise she bumped into Daisy Quantock coming out.

"Daisy! What are you doing here, not thinking of moving to Tilling are you? It would be too much of a coincidence."

Daisy gave her a quick peck on the cheek. "Well Lucia as a matter of fact I am. Robert and I have decided we've had enough of Riseholme and have always liked Tilling so I thought I'll have a look at what was available. Unfortunately I couldn't find anything I liked in the estate agents so it's been a wasted journey."

"Never mind. Where are you staying? You can stay with us at *Mallards* if you like. Georgie will be pleased to see you it will cheer him up. I just need to pop into the estate agent myself to see how much they want for the house next door to us."

Daisy looked surprised, "they didn't show me that, I'll go back in with you."

An hour later they were having tea in *Mallards* sitting room. Georgie had yet to make an appearance and Lucia explained to Daisy what had happened. "Shall I go up do you think?" Daisy asked.

"No leave him he'll come down when he gets hungry. Now what about this house next door?"

"I liked the look of it from the outside but it doesn't appear to be on the market."

"Elizabeth was looking at it this morning so she must know something. I'll ask Diva tomorrow she's sure to know."

Georgie was lying on his bed, he'd been feeling very upset all morning, he'd tried rearranging his bibelots but without much enthusiasm so he just lay down feeling sorry for himself. At about eleven he heard Lucia returning with someone downstairs. He'd pressed his ear to the door but couldn't make out who she was talking to. He decided he was too upset to think about but by twelve o'clock feeling rather hungry, he decided to put on a brave face and go down. When he entered the sitting room he was pleased to see it was Daisy he'd heard, 'she'll understand how I feel,' he thought to himself.

***

Diva was busy with Janet setting up her tea shop for the next day. She'd done very well over the last few days and was ready to put her feet up. As she was about to lock the door Elizabeth burst in looking excited over something.

"It's ideal!" She said.

"What is? Look Elizabeth I've had a busy day and need to rest so just get on with it."

"Yes. Yes, of course Diva dear always so busy, but I just had to tell you how much I liked Mrs Ames's old house. Why isn't it on the market I wonder?"

"I heard that they can't contact the next of kin. I did go and see Mrs Ames when she moved in, just to be neighbourly you know, and she told me she had moved here from Riseborough after her husband died. She said she had a son but there was a falling out over a woman or something, she was a bit vague. Anyway, that's all I know so if you don't mind Janet and I need to get on."

"I do need to find out who owns the house if I'm to buy it, anyway, thank you Diva always so helpful, I'll leave you both in peace." As she walked back to *Grebe*, Elizabeth resolved to go to Riseborough the very next day and see if she could find the son Diva had mentioned.

3.

Over the next week Lucia started taking her driving lessons. Daisy had only stayed the one night and Lucia promised to contact her as soon as she had spoken to Diva. The truth was she'd put this off as she'd met Major Benjy on the high street the next day who told her that

Elizabeth had gone away for a few days to speak to the owner of the house and find out when they were likely to sell, so she decided to make learning to drive a priority. She'd had six lessons by the end of the week and Cadman said she was doing very well and should apply for her test soon. She hadn't told anyone she was learning to drive but word had got around as she spotted Diva driving an old black Ford two days before and Friday morning, as she was doing her shopping, Elizabeth drove past with Cadman in their Jaguar.

"Well she's back from her travels and hasn't wasted time contacting Cadman I see," Lucia said to Georgie as they strolled along the high street. At that moment, Diva emerged from Mr Twistevant's shop.

"Got a new car Diva?"

"No Lucia it's an old thing, I thought I'd better give it a few runs, you know, to see if it's still OK before I exchange it for a new model."

"I never knew you had a car, kept that quiet. Anyway, I'm please I've caught you, I wondered if you knew if Elizabeth had found out who owns Mrs Ames's old house as Daisy Quantock is interested in it?"

Diva told her that Elizabeth had indeed found out and that Mr Ames, her son, had moved to Tilling a few years ago.

Elizabeth called on him as soon as she returned from Riseborough. He lived in a small terraced house near the station. He told her he'd moved there to be near his mother and that he'd yet to sort out what to do about her house. Elizabeth didn't stay long as he seemed a little the 'worse for wear' she thought. He did say he would visit the estate agent the next day and arrange things.

Diva related all this information to Lucia who immediately called at Woolgar and Pipstow where they informed her that Mr Ames had called round and the house was to be auctioned next week.

\*\*\*

It was a bright March morning and Georgie was feeling much better. He was getting over the upset about Foljambe who had stayed for a few weeks to show Lucia the routines. Since then Lucia had been especially attentive, making sure he had all he needed and generally fussing round him. This morning he had dressed in this brightest jacket with a large hat to match in an effort to cheer himself up. On his way down the High Street he met Quaint Irene who'd just returned from America with her friend.

"You look as splendid as ever Georgie, I'd like you to meet Tammy who's over from America for a few weeks."

"Nice to meet you, what an unusual name," he said taking in her bright coloured suit.

"Not in America. You look very smart," she replied with a smile.

"I hear everyone's taken up driving," Irene said.

"Yes it's a tar'some nuisance, the High Street was full enough with Wyse's Royce but now we have Elizabeth racing about learning to drive and even Diva has dug out her old car."

At that moment with a series of bangs and black smoke Diva drove past in the old Ford. It sounded barely road worthy as it rattled past.

"I see what you mean, I shall have to start driving again, I'm getting rusty. We hear there's to be an Easter Parade that sounds jolly."

Elizabeth appeared with her shopping bag on her arm and hurried over. "How nice to see you back again quaint one, did you enjoy yourself in America? I see you've brought a nice friend back with you…"

"No car today?" Georgie said interrupting her.

"No naughty Benjy has taken it to the golf course I really needed to get another couple of lessons in before my test. Lucia has her test soon, such a good driver, I'm sure she'll pass with flying colours."

"I hear that you and Major Benjy are moving house." said Georgie

"Yes, we want to live closer to all our dear friends. We are going to bid on the house next door to you."

"Good luck on that, isn't Daisy Quantock also in the running," said Georgie "plenty of money as well by all accounts."

"Ah dear Daisy so nice if she could move to Tilling but Benjy and I have our hearts set on that house and you know how determined Benjy can be."

"You mean you Mapp," quipped Irene "let the best man win I say!"

Suddenly they heard Diva's car give another loud bang as it came to a stop with a judder in the middle of the road. She struggled out slammed the door gave it a kick and came hurrying down to join in the group.

"Well that's it the old thing has packed up, I'm done with cars too much trouble. Have I missed anything?"

"No Diva that **would** be a first, well must get on so much to do, au reservoir," Elizabeth said as she hurried into the post office.

"What was that she said?" asked Tammy

"Nothing, she's always saying it, copies Lucia and who can blame her?" Said Irene

\*\*\*

Meanwhile, Lucia was sitting in the garden room waiting for Georgie to return. She had invited Daisy and Robert to stay at *Mallards* until the auction and had finally decided on a plan to ensure Elizabeth didn't win at the auction. As soon as Georgie came in, she outlined her strategy.

"Now listen, I've got a plan. You must go to the auction and outbid Elizabeth."

"Lucia! Outbid her! How, I've never been to an auction I wouldn't know what to do."

"Don't be silly Georgie there's nothing to it you just stick your hand up at the right time, don't worry I'll go through it all with you before you go."

"Why can't you do it Lucia, you'd be much better than me I'm sure to get it wrong."

"I can't go Elizabeth would suspect straight away if I appeared, no you must go in disguise."

"Disguise! Everyone will know it's me as soon as I speak."

"You don't have to speak don't worry we'll go through it this afternoon, the auction isn't for a few days so we have plenty of time to practise your role, now Georgie let's have lunch and we'll sort this out properly later."

Georgie wasn't happy about the plan but the thought of wearing a disguise did sound exciting and he began to think of what he might wear.

"Perhaps my long Burberry overcoat with a large red hat would be nice or I could blend in better if I wore my Harris Tweed jacket, I don't really like it and haven't worn it much so no-one will recognise me. Oh dear what a worry it all is." he thought.

4.

The day of the auction had arrived, Daisy and Robert had stayed overnight at *Mallards* and were getting ready to go. They hadn't really decided on tactics so when Lucia said at breakfast they should have a plan they were thrown into confusion. She said they must decide to outbid Elizabeth whatever happened and they agreed with this, they were sure there wouldn't be a problem as they were getting a good price for their house in Riseholme and so they felt everything would be fine. Even though he had never been to an auction, Robert had read up about it and felt he knew the conventions to follow.

Back in the bedroom as they got ready they began to worry again.

"We must make sure we get this house I've set my heart on it," said Daisy

"Yes dear but we mustn't be too hasty we don't want to pay too much for it, from what you say it sounds as though it needs a lot of work."

"Robert but if Elizabeth wins I don't know what we'll do. Anyway, let's set off so we can get a good seat."

Georgie was also worried, he'd discussed tactics with Lucia last evening and she'd dismissed all his disguises as unsuitable.

"You can't wear any of those coats they would stand out too much here put on this black coat of mine and let's see."

Georgie tried it on, it was a little short in the sleeves but otherwise seemed to just about fit even though it buttoned up the wrong way.

"Well I had thought of something more stylish but I suppose no-one will notice me in this, I can wear my old black hat with it."

"Yes and sunglasses."

"What, in the winter? Won't it look strange?"

"No Georgie it will help the disguise. Now you know what to do. If Daisy is winning don't do anything, you only need to bid if they have stopped and Elizabeth is about to win, are you certain you understand, perhaps I'd better come and make sure."

"No Lucia it will be fine I'm sure I won't need to get involved, Daisy and Robert are really eager to win."

Lucia looked up and down the street to see if the coast was clear. "Come on Georgie if you go now you won't be seen.'

Georgie looked round the front door, 'Oh Lucia I don't think I can do it I'm all of a shake, why do we have to be so secretive?"

"Georgie, if Elizabeth finds out it's us that lost her the house we would never hear the last of it, you know what she's like. If we do it in secret, then no-one will be able to say who the buyer was and we can sort things out with Daisy later."

"Oh very well but I'm still worried we'll be found out."

He off started down the road towards the auction hall, jumping at every shadow. As luck would have it most of the town's people were already in the hall so he met no-one along the way. When he entered the hall, he could see the Mapp-Flints at the front and not far behind were Daisy and Robert. Over to his right was Quaint Irene with her new friend and he spotted the Wyses and Diva in the crowd near the front. Luckily no-one was looking at him as he sat at the back and waited for the bidding to start. There were several smaller properties up first and they were dealt with very quickly.

"Now for lot number 6; *Firsdown*," said the auctioneer.

Georgie wasn't taking much notice at the time as he'd suddenly realised that he'd put on his brown shoes in the hurry and they looked terrible with the black coat. He was in the process of deciding whether to pop back home and change when he noticed that Benjy had started bidding.

"So *Firsdown* must be the name of the house next door. Strange as there were no fir trees anywhere near,' he thought.

The bidding proceeded and had reached £1000. Robert bid £1200 and Benjy upped it to £1400. The auction was silent for a moment as the auctioneer looked round the hall for further bids. 'Oh dear' thought Georgie 'should I bid now?' He decided to wait a little longer to see what Robert did. The auctioneer started to raise the gavel when Robert suddenly bid £1600. Georgie could see the Mapp-Flints whispering to each other and eventually they bid £1800. There was another silence and the auctioneer said, "are there anymore bids?" No-one replied Daisy was looking at Robert who was shaking his head. The auctioneer had raised his gavel and was just about to hammer it down when Georgie held up his hand.

"A new bidder, £2000!" Shouted the auctioneer "are there any more?..." Everyone seemed to hold their breath, Daisy and Robert were looking at each other but didn't make a move. "Going, going, gone. Sold to the gentleman at the back of the room."

Everyone immediately looked round but Georgie just had time to slip from the hall before anyone saw him. He went round by the side passage to give his name to the clerk who was sitting behind a screen.

"Don't give my name out if anyone asks." He said. That done he raced home to tell Lucia the result.

"Oh dear £2000 how will we pay it? Oh dear what a mess," he thought as he hurried up the street.

Lucia was waiting for him when he arrived back. "Well?" she said.

"We won the house for £2000! Oh Lucia what will we do we don't have that much money."

Lucia had already considered this possibility and had decided already on a plan. "We'll rent the house to Daisy and Robert, this will help to pay for any loan we may need."

"Will they want it do you think?"

"We'll ask them, I can hear them arriving back now."

They both entered the sitting room looking decidedly miserable. "We didn't get the house," said Robert.

"No, we did," said Lucia. "Now before you say anything. we did it because needed to stop Elizabeth moving next door. I love Her and Benjy but to have them next door would have been too much for me. Georgie was at the auction and able to bid just in time. What we planned was for you to rent the house from us until you had decided what to do next about moving."

"Well this is a surprise," said Daisy "yes of course we could rent it but the truth is we took too long deciding whether to bid. We can afford it really so how about we buy it from you instead?"

5

Elizabeth hadn't been out of the house for two days, she was so angry, she didn't feel able to see anyone. Major Benjy had disappeared to the golf course to get out of the way as usual. That morning she'd nagged him again to find out who had won the house but to no avail. So she decided she needed to do something herself. She went, firstly, to the auctioneer's but they told her in no uncertain terms that the buyer had expressly asked for his name to be kept anonymous. She then tried the estate agent with no better success. She called on Diva to find that she had already left to go shopping. So she hurried down the High Street to find her or someone who had been at the auction to see if they had recognised the bidder. The first person she saw was Quaint Irene.

"Well dear Irene what a fiasco that auction was, I don't suppose you were able to see who the buyer was?"

"No Mapp we were near the front. Looks like you're stuck at *Grebe* for a bit longer."

"I couldn't be more annoyed and to cap it all I managed to fail my driving test that same afternoon. Such a stupid examiner said I hadn't done this and I'd forgot to do that, really I drove perfectly well given I was in such a bad mood."

"Never mind Mapp you can take it again."

"Oh, I won't be doing that such a waste of time, I don't know what possessed me to bother driving, Benjy can drive anyway. I blame Lucia stirring up all the enthusiasm."

"Really Mapp she did no such thing, she's been perfectly marvellous. She must have passed her test because I saw her driving on her own this morning."

Diva emerged from Mr Twistevants at that moment, "whoever bought *Firsdown* is moving in, I saw the furniture arriving."

Elizabeth nearly dropped her shopping basket.

"Right!" She said "we'll soon find out who the new owner is. Come on."

All three of them hurried up the road to see what was happening. When they arrived, there was a large removal van being unloaded outside the house. A table and four chairs were being carried in followed by bust of Apollo. Suddenly Daisy rushed out of the door with a broom in her hand shouting, "be careful with that it's very valuable!"

"Daisy!" Elizabeth called "you, how is it that you've bought the house you were outbid?"

"I've no time to talk Elizabeth I've got so much to do," with that she disappeared inside again.

Elizabeth was furious and was just about to go in and confront her when Lucia appeared. She had a bright scarf tied round her head and a large feather duster in her hand.

"That house should have been mine and Benjy's. We've been tricked out of it."

"The bidding was fair and square by all accounts." Lucia replied.

"How could it be? Daisy wasn't the highest bidder." Elizabeth shouted back.

Diva and Irene were enjoying the drama of it, Irene shouted, "give up Mapp you lost!"

Lucia came over to them, "look Elizabeth, all you need to know is that a deal was made and the house is now Robert and Daisy's so why don't you come and help us clean up it's rather a mess inside."

"As much as I'd love to help you and dear Daisy, I haven't time I've so much to do now we've decided to stay at *Grebe*," she said with a forced smile. "Do give my love to Robert and Daisy, it will be nice to have them living at Tilling, tell them I shall invite them to my next bridge evening, au reservoir."

"She's putting on a brave face," said Diva watching her go. "After all, what else can she do?"

\*\*\*

Things had quietened down after moving day and Elizabeth had been seen about the town as usual, shopping and chatting with people along the way. In fact, back to her old self. When she saw Daisy on the high street a week later, she asked her how she was settling in, "nicely I hope," she said with one of her 'winning' smiles. "Benjy and I are quite pleased not to have won the house we feel we would like something a little more modern. Such a problem these old houses always needing repairs to be done. Still, Daisy dear, I'm sure you'll manage, Robert is so handy I hear."

"Yes, Elizabeth everything is going well and we are looking forward to the Easter Parade on Sunday."

"Oh yes such fun, dear Lucia always doing something or other, still, can't stop and chat must get on."

6.

Sunday came and Lucia had been busy all morning. Her hat for the Easter Parade needed some finishing touches and she'd been on the phone to the Mayor for an hour making sure that everything was in place and ready to go at 2.00pm. Georgie was being particularly difficult, insisting on wearing a bright yellow jacket and hat which made him look like 'a bowl of custard' Lucia told him but he said it was just right for Easter and intended to add a few daffodils from the garden to his button hole. The padre had called round worried that not everyone would be able to fit in the church. The Mayor had told him they expected half the town to turn up. Lucia did her best to reassure him that it would be fine and anyway they could leave the door open so that the people outside would hear the service. It was clear that he wasn't convinced but decided it was the only thing they could do. The weather was bright if a little windy so Lucia was sure that the event would be a great success.

Georgie, meanwhile, was reconsidering his outfit "how I wish Foljambe were here to offer advice," he thought "perhaps the yellow is a little too much."

In the end he decided to tone it down with a dark red scarf and matching trousers. "That should be fine and I'll abandon the daffodils to please Lucia."

By 1.30pm people had started arriving at the town hall. Daisy and Robert had been the first there and Daisy was carefully arranging her new hat to look its best. She'd bought a simple brown felt hat and created a spring scene out of cloth and raffia on it, depicting a lamb standing in a field of grass with some small crocuses around it. It was attached to the hat with wire. She thought it made a striking impression even though the hat looked rather perched on her head. Robert hated it but said nothing, they had been having a busy time cleaning and moving furniture so he didn't want any more upset.

Within a few minutes, Diva arrived with the Wyses. Diva's hat was one she had worn before with a bit of extra yellow ribbon but Mrs Wyse had excelled herself with a creation of silk and paste jewellery resulting in a startling array of colours and glitter. They hadn't long to wait before Lucia and Georgie arrived, Georgie dazzling everyone with his yellow outfit and Lucia's hat was a nice arrangement of bows and artificial flowers. She had arranged for the local brass band to lead the parade and they were busy tuning up.

"Are we all here?" she asked looking round.

"Here's Quaint Irene with her friend but no sign of the Mapp-Flints yet," said Diva.

Irene and Tammy wore the same style of hat, boater shaped with the stars and stripes round the rim and a small American flag on the top.

"Hope you like our efforts, Lucia darling," Irene said, "brought them back with us from America so just right for today don't you think?"

"Um very nice Irene, now come on everyone get in line," she said as Evie Bartlett and the Padre arrived 'we can't wait all day."

Just as they were moving off Elizabeth and Major Benjy turned up, "hope we're not late," she said as she pushed Benjy into line near the front. Her hat was an odd shape and looked rather like a small parasol with flowers poking out and some ribbons underneath that were mostly covered over. Benjy looked very smart in this uniform and carried his golfing umbrella like a sword which tended to poke anyone who stood too close.

The band started up and they set off at a brisk pace. Towards the back were the town's tradespeople including Mr Twistevant and Dodo from the sweet shop. Taking up the rear were the Boy Scout troop and representative from the various sports and social groups in the town. It wasn't too far to the church and there was an admiring crowd to cheer them on who then joined the parade as it passed. All was going well and Lucia could see the church up ahead.

"I do believe I felt a drop of rain" she said to Georgie as they neared the church yard.

"Oh how tar'some, I hope we get in before it starts."

The band started to quicken up as the rain persisted and by the time they had reached the church gate it was raining quite hard. At the door, the band leader insisted they all go in as the rain would damage the instruments. It had been planned that they stayed in the church yard and play to everyone as they passed. Getting the band into the church caused a hold-up and by the time Lucia and Georgie managed to get inside they were wet through. Lucia's hat was a disaster and she thrust it under the pew as she sat down.

Everyone arrived drenched, with their hats destroyed by the rain. Most of the townspeople had hurried home as soon as the rain started and only the Boy Scouts and Dodo from the sweet shop were left to push in at the back. She was carrying a basket of little Easter Eggs as a reward for the scouts and didn't want them to get ruined.

Everyone had settled down in their damp clothes when the church door opened again and Elizabeth and Benjy appeared. Benjy had used his umbrella to shelter Elizabeth and he folded it up and stood at the side of the pews. Elizabeth hurried to the front and squeezed into a small space between Daisy and Lucia. She was completely dry and her hat was a triumph. It was made up of a small disc that she'd fixed to an old hat but she had covered it with ribbon and artificial spring flowers that she spread out in an array of colour.

"I expect that was such a nice hat when you set off," she whispered to Daisy "but the rain has done it no favours. Still you've been too busy to bother with it no doubt, doing all the work on that old house you managed to acquire."

"Make some room Elizabeth," Daisy snapped "you don't get any smaller you know."

"What a large turnout a credit to your wonderful organisation as usual," Elizabeth said turning to Lucia. "I do hope you soon dry out, the good thing about living at *Grebe* is you get to know when it's going to rain, Benjy's a positive weather guru these days, aren't you Benjy?" She shouted over "such a treasure."

"If you say so old girl. I'm used to the rain anyway; did I ever tell you about the time the Jumna was in flood…"

To everyone's relief the organ started to play the first hymn.

The End

## Mapp and Lucia aloft

The Padre was in a state. When he'd arrived at the church that morning he'd noticed some broken tiles lying on the ground at the side of the church. He hurried over to see where they had fallen from and when he looked up at the roof he could make out some of the lead flashing had been removed. As he stood further back he realised that all the lead on that part of the roof had been stolen. Lucia was passing the church when the Padre came running round the corner shouting about the theft.

"Mrs Pillson contact Mrs Wyse at once and see what we have in the roof fund. We will need to sort this out quickly", he said as he hurried into the vestry to call the local police.

That done he thought the best thing would be to go to the Town Hall and speak to the Mayor and ask him what could be done.

"Now calm down Padre and tell me what the problem is" said the Mayor leading by the arm him to a nearby chair.

"It's a disaster Mayor, we've had a robbery. Oh dear, what a calamity!"

"A robbery! How awful! Whatever has been taken?"

"Lead, Mayor, lead from the roof it's terrible we are in need of work already to replace old tiles and guttering but now with the lead gone the rain will pour in and ruin everything, I don't know what we'll do".

The Mayor sat down next to him "Have you any idea who took it?"

"No, there has been several such thefts in the area and they usually happen at night. They can sell the lead for high sums you know."

"What can we do about it? Have you any money in the roof fund for repairs?"

"Very little, Mayor. Mrs Wyse has been looking after it for us but we really need to set about raising more and soon if we are to save the church. I've asked Mrs Pillson to contact her at once".

As soon as Lucia returned home she rang Susan Wyse and explained what had happened

"There is very little money left, I'm afraid," she said. "We spent quite a lot on the new window last year. We really must start and raise some more."

Lucia had been involved in a few campaigns around jumble sales and fetes and she knew that Susan had also been raising money. In fact, there had been an item in the local paper about her good works but much of this money had not been spent on the roof as planned but used to pay for a much-needed window replacement

"We must start soon because, now the lead's stolen, the rain's sure to get in. We should call a meeting to plan tactics." Susan said, "I'll arrange one for tomorrow in the school hall".

As she put the phone down Georgie came into the garden room. He had woken up late and only just finished breakfast.

"What's all the fuss, who was on the phone?"

"Georgie the Padre's in a terrible state the lead's been stolen from the church roof. I've just spoken to Susan and we're having a meeting to try and raise some funds."

"Oh dear how tar'some. Whatever do they want lead for?"

"I don't know Georgie but I think it's valuable and they sell it. Susan said she'd call a meeting tomorrow. We must both go and see what we can do to help."

\*\*\*

A well-attended meeting was held the next evening in the school hall. As Lucia walked in, she spotted Diva Plaistow and Elizabeth Mapp-Flint sitting together on the front row.

"Quiet please," said the Mayor from the stage "we are here to think of ways to raise some urgent funds to repair the church roof. I expect you've all heard that the lead has been stolen. The police are looking into the matter but we need to get the fund raising started at once, has anyone any ideas?"

"How about a raffle or another jumble sale?" suggested Diva.

"Oh Diva!" Said Elizabeth "we need to do something that gets lots of money, the last jumble sale only raised about twenty pounds."

"I think a raffle might be a start" said Susan, "I'll sort that out tomorrow."

"I say we let the church fall down and give the money to people who need it," shouted Quaint Irene from the back "who cares about the roof!"

"Yes quaint one you would say that," said Elizabeth climbing onto the stage in front of the Mayor "now if you shout out ideas I'll write them on the blackboard."

"I'm happy to arrange a church fete, if that's a help." Said Daisy Quantock.

"Good." Said Elizabeth writing it up and putting Daisy's name by it.

While this was happening, Major Benjy had been sitting quietly at the side. He had been dragged to the meeting by Elizabeth but hoped to get away to the Kings Arms for a few pints as soon as possible. While he listened to the suggestions he remembered a conversation he'd had at the golf club a few days ago which he thought might hurry the meeting along. "There's this groundsman at the golf club," he said standing up, "has a large hot air balloon, I'm told he gives people rides in it, perhaps we could make a sign and fly round the area so that everyone knew about the problem and where to donate."

"That might be a good idea," said the Padre.

"Oh do sit down Benjy, it's a ridiculous idea who's going to go up in a balloon?" Asked Elizabeth with a sigh.

"I would!" Volunteered Lucia "it may not be as bizarre as it sounds, if we pinned a big sign on it asking for donations people will be sure give something."

"I'll speak to the groundsman tomorrow and sort something out. Now, if we've finished I've an important job in hand," said Benjy as he began to head for the door.

"Hold on!" Shouted Elizabeth from the stage, knowing full well where he was off to. "We will need to plan this properly it could take a while."

"I'll leave it with you Liz," he said disappearing out the door.

\*\*\*

Elizabeth made sure that Major Benjy spoke to the groundsman the very next day and he brought the balloon to the school yard on Saturday morning as arranged. A small group of people were arriving to watch it being inflated. The groundsman had enlisted the help of Cadman and they were busy hauling the balloon into place as the people watched.

"This is a prototype really, I inherited it from my father who made it," the groundsman said as he fixed the ropes to the basket, "I've given people rides all over the countryside but this type of balloon is not common you know." The groundsman had lit the burner earlier that morning so as people watched the balloon began to inflate quite rapidly.

Elizabeth had been one of the first to arrive and she was followed a few minutes after by Lucia and Georgie. Lucia had made the effort to dress in what she decided was appropriate for ballooning. A smart suit and large hat with a feather, which she felt look would well in a balloon. Georgie had also made an effort, wearing a long red cape with gold trimmings. He made sure he chose one with a hood as he was worried about his hair in the wind.

"No Major Benjy this morning?" Asked Lucia.

"No, he's a little under the weather, I'm afraid, coming down with something I think. I left him sitting over a bowl of porridge."

"Oh dear I am sorry," said Georgie "he looked alright at the meeting the other day."

To Elizabeth's relief the groundsman came over at that moment. "I will now need someone in the basket to help with the stove."

"I'll do it," said Elizabeth quickly to avoid further questioning about Benjy's health. The groundsman helped her climb up a small step ladder into the basket.

"Now the stove is inflating the balloon, the valve is on the top there and you must open and close it when I say. Use the glove as it's hot."

In fact the balloon was beginning to look quite impressive already. A large banner had been attached to the side of the basket calling for donations at the town hall and it was brightly coloured and eye catching so Lucia thought it should do the job.

"Oh dear, I'm not sure how to do this," said Elizabeth. "Do I open it here?" She pointed vaguely at the metal plate.

"Let me see," said Lucia climbing up the ladder. As her skirt was rather tight, the groundsman had to help her in.

"Thank you... I'm afraid I don't know your name."

"It's Mellors," he said with a smile.

"Thank you Mellors. I've sure I've heard that name before.... Oh yes I remember! And you're just as I imagined when I read the book." She said wryly.

He clearly didn't know what she was referring to. "Don't worry about the valve," he said "leave it for now, it's inflating well. I will need to get some sandbags from the van to act as ballast. Give me a hand will you Mr Cadman?"

"It is a grand sight," said Georgie. "Why it's almost off the ground already. Oh look! The rope is coming loose, I'd better do something otherwise it will float away."

"Hurry Georgie it's beginning to rise up quite quickly," shouted Lucia.

Georgie grabbed the long rope attached to the basket and pulled it over to the school railings.

"Oh the tar'some thing, it's too thick I can't tie it". He found that the balloon was in fact beginning to pull him along as he spoke. "I need to keep hold or you'll fly away Lucia," he shouted as he slid along the ground. He looked frantically around for Mellors but he was still busy unloading sacks from his van. Suddenly, there was a gust of wind and the balloon rose up into the air lifting Georgie off his feet.

"Georgie!" Cried Lucia looking over the side of the basket "I think you'll have to let go or you'll be carried away."

At that moment, Major Benjy, who had decided to leave his breakfast and go for a walk to clear his head, entered the playground and spotted Georgie being lifted from the ground. He ran over to try and catch him. Mellors had also noticed what was happening.

"Quickly grab his legs," he shouted to Major Benjy. It was difficult as Benjy had to jump, but he just managed to grab hold of Georgie's feet in time. Georgie realising he couldn't hold on to the rope with one hand and his hair with the other let go and with a weak cry of "Help!" tumbled down landing on top of Major Benjy, knocking him over.

"Georgie, are you all right!" Shouted Lucia. She could see the two of them struggling on the ground. Mellors tried to jump for the dangling rope but by now it was well out of reach. "Close the valve on the stove" he shouted.

Georgie managed, with Major Benjy's help, to get to his feet, "what a good job you were there to save me," he said pulling his hood straight.

"No problem old boy," replied Benjy giving Georgie a slap on the back which almost knocked him over again. Georgie looked up at the receding balloon. "What are we to do they're floating away?"

"We'll follow them in the van and hopefully they'll work out how to bring it down safely," said Mellors.

***

Elizabeth had decided she was going to die. She sat on the floor of the basket and refused to move.

"I can't bear to look over the side. I go all giddy. This is another fine mess you've got me into," she said sounding to Lucia a bit like Oliver Hardy.

"Elizabeth, it was you who got into the basket first."

"Yes but I didn't expect it to leave the ground, it's floating up and up, we'll never get it down again."

"Don't be silly it's something to do with this stove thing over here, if I close the plate on the top it might bring help. Mellors shouted something about it as we left the school yard."

"Try that then, anything to get us down."

Lucia pushed the plate over but as it was hot she misjudged it and knocked it over the side of the basket. "Ouch! It's hot and now it's fallen."

"Well done, you should have used the gloves, that's it then we'll end up at sea again for sure." Said Elizabeth mopping her brow with a handkerchief.

Lucia looked over the side and saw they had floated away from the school and were over some fields heading towards the beach, "they'll have to call out the coast guards. I'm sure we'll be alright."

As they floated on Elizabeth tried to work out what was the best thing to do. "If only we could cover the stove it would be fine, the hot air would stop going into the balloon and we would sail down again." She had a sudden idea. "Give me your hat Lucia."

"What, it will never suit you you're much too short to wear a large hat like this."

"I'm not going to wear it, just give it to me," she grabbed it from Lucia and put it over the stove "there that will stop the heat raising."

"Elizabeth that's my best hat and what's more it'll catch fire."

56

"Yes, it might but there's nothing else we can use so we'll just have to take that chance."

In fact, it did seem to be working the balloon began to descend a little.

"We can't set down here it's all rocks," shouted Lucia looking over the side "we need to reach the fields again."

"Try pulling on that rope dangling from the top it might help us to change direction."

As luck would have it the wind began to blow them in-land a little and as Lucia pulled on the rope the balloon did seem to veer round slightly.

"Watch out for that pylon!" Shouted Elizabeth. "Take your hat off the stove, quickly".

Lucia pulled the scorched hat to the floor and the balloon began to rise again, just high enough to miss the wires.

"That was close we could have been electrocuted, the sooner we get off this wretched balloon the better," said Elizabeth.

Lucia retrieved the ruined hat from the floor and covered the stove again.

"We're heading toward *Grebe*, I can see it in front of us." said Elizabeth standing up "perhaps we could land in the garden."

"The garden! Don't be silly Elizabeth it's much too small. Look there are two men on the roof, they must be there to help us. They could save us by grabbing the rope as we pass." As they drifted closer it was clear that the men weren't there for them at all. They hadn't even noticed the balloon coming towards them.

"There're doing something to the roof," said Lucia

"Yes they are, they're stealing the lead!" Shouted Elizabeth waving her arms at them. As the balloon got nearer the men suddenly noticed it and started to climb over to a ladder that they'd propped up the side of the house. The balloon was level with the roof by now and as the men reached the ladder it scraped the tiles and hit one of the men knocking him into the garden. The other man managed to reach the ground and, as they floated away, they could see him climbing into a lorry and driving off.

They were beginning to float upwards again and Lucia saw that the hat had almost burnt through. "Now what can we do! Look at my best hat, ruined." she said, pulling the remains off the stove.

\*\*\*

Mellors drove the van along the road trying to keep the balloon in sight.

"It's going towards the coast," said Georgie, "we should try to get to the beach road."

"No wait!" Shouted Major Benjy leaning out of the van window. "It's turned inland. They just missed a pylon and it's heading towards *Grebe*. Down here Mellors," he said pointing to a side road.

"Oh dear, I'm getting car sick all this jolting about. I'll have to get out," said Georgie.

"We can't stop we'll lose them," said Mellors, "and there's a lorry coming up the road at quite a pace."

He pulled the van over to let the lorry pass. Georgie was just about to climb out when they set off again.

"By Jove! The balloon's heading for the golf course," shouted Benjy. "Turn up here, they may be able to land on the green."

As they drew near to the golf course Georgie, who had forgotten about his sickness, spotted Mr and Mrs Wyse walking up to the club house. As they drew near, Mellors stopped the van and quickly told them about the balloon. They agreed to watch out for it in case it came into land.

"Perhaps we could have a quick one in the club bar while we wait?" Suggested Benjy.

"No time for that," said Georgie "they're almost here." As he spoke he could see the balloon heading towards them over the rise of the hill.

Mr and Mrs Wyse had also spotted it and ran to a high point on the green to see if they could halt its progress by grabbing the trailing rope. By now the balloon had descended a little and Lucia could be seen waving to them from the basket.

"When they get overhead we must try to catch hold of the rope," said Mellors.

The five of them stood together in the balloon's path.

"Get on my back Mr Pillson and see if you can grab it," But before Georgie could reply Mellors had hoisted him up and onto his shoulders.

"I'm no good at this, Mellors, grabbing ropes has never been my sort of thing you know. I'm quite butter fingered really."

"Oh do shut up Pillson and get on with it," shouted Benjy "why in the Punjab I was grabbing ropes all the time nothing to it!"

As the balloon came nearer, to Georgie's relief he could see that the rope was almost touching the ground so Mellors lifted him down and they all ran to grab it at once, banging into each other and generally falling over. Luckily Mellors ran ahead and quickly caught hold of the rope. With Mr Wyse's help they pulled the balloon over to the van and tied it securely to the fender.

"Oh Mellor's you're wonderful," shouted Lucia from the basket "now help me get out of here."

Without the ladder is was a struggle but she managed to climber over the side and drop into Mellors' arms. "Thank you Mellors you're so strong."

"Do let go of him Lucia," Georgie said, "he's to get Elizabeth down yet."

So far no one had sight of Elizabeth but on hearing her name she popped up and looked over the side of the basket. "Benjy, please get me down, I never want to see a balloon again."

When they were all safely on the ground Benjy suggested they all go for a quick pick-me-up in the club house and to his surprise, everyone agreed. Mellors said he'd stay to secure the balloon properly. "Leave it with me, I'll take it up and sail round with the sign later."
***
Lucia was sitting in the garden room with Georgie, a week later thinking about her flight in the balloon. She'd decided to hold a little musical evening to celebrate the success of the 'balloon adventure', as she called it. "Georgie, we must play something lively and victorious."

"I can't think of anything, how about 'Land of hope and glory'? Everyone likes that and they can all join in."

"No Georgie too strident, not at all suitable, I'll see what else we have," she said, looking through the sheet music. The Padre had called earlier to say that they'd raised over two hundred pounds so far and what's more, he told them, the police had caught the men involved. One was in hospital after his fall from *Grebe*'s roof.

"Mellors has been very good giving people rides in his balloon at ten shillings each and Susan raised about thirty pounds with her raffle. What was the prize?" Georgie asked

"A ride in the balloon I think. Yes, Mellors was wonderful the way he caught me when I jumped from the basket, Georgie did you see?"

"I saw you making a fool of yourself."

"Don't be silly Georgie I was just grateful we all survived unharmed."

"I still can't understand how you got the balloon to descend without the stove cover."

"Well Georgie, it was all down to Elizabeth, she managed to cover it with one of her undergarments. I think it best if we keep quiet about it though, to avoid embarrassment, don't you?"

"Yes, yes, I wish I'd not asked now! Anyway, all I can say is let's not go ballooning again. Ever!" said Georgie.

**The End**

## Diva's dilemma

It had all started in mid-July when Elizabeth Mapp-Flint was visiting the local estate agents, Woolgar and Pipstow. She had instructed them to find a tenant for *Grebe* over the summer period and to her surprise they informed her that one had already been found. A Colonel Shyton had put a deposit down and wanted to move in at once for six weeks. Elizabeth was delighted but now she had to face the problem of finding somewhere for Major Benjy and herself to stay. As she left the estate agent's office she tried to think about the option open to her. She immediately ruled Wasters out now it was 'Ye Olde Tea-house'. Diva had already informed her that the summer was her busiest time and letting the house was out of the question. She had approached Daisy Quantock earlier by phone but received a curt refusal. "Much too busy moving in," was the reply. 'Must be the longest "moving in" in history' she thought to herself. The Wyse's and Lucia's houses would be much too expensive, so she was at a loss to know what to do. Although it wasn't ideal, as a last resort, she decided to drop in on Quaint Irene to see if Taormina was available. She wasn't too keen as it was usually full of artist's material all strewn about the place. The door was answered by Irene's intimidating maid, Lucy.

"She's not in!" was the answer to Elizabeth's enquiry. "Gone to Folkestone, won't be back till Wednesday," and with that she shut the door in Elizabeth's face.

Lucia and Georgie were sitting in the Garden Room sorting through sheet music as usual. Lucia wasn't fully involved with the task as she had just received upsetting news from the Mayor who had called round to tell her that the Town Hall would not be available for the annual art exhibition. They were having it redecorated, he informed her, while the Town Council were on holiday and, as there were no other suitable venues, he felt the event should be called off.

"Well Georgie' I'm most upset" she said throwing the sheet music down "I'd been asked to join the hanging committee again this year as the Wyses and Irene will be away, and now it turns out that there won't be a committee to join."

"What a shame, I'd planned to finish my set of water colours, 'The Streets of Tilling'. I've got two done and hoped to get another two finished by the time of the exhibition."

"There'll be a few disappointed people. Diva said that Irene's going to Folkestone to paint some seascapes. What they'll look like is anyone's guess but I'm sure she'd want to show them at the exhibition. It's an important date on the Tilling calendar every year, a great loss."

"Why don't we have it here, Lucia? We could make room perhaps?"

"I had thought about it but some of the paintings are quite big, I've seen Mr Wye's canvas, and I doubt we'd get it in the door, never mind find wall space. Perhaps the Padre will have some ideas? We could use the church I suppose, I'll call round and see him later."


Quaint Irene returned from Folkestone on Tuesday night and was busy sorting her painting equipment, ready for going away when Lucy announced, "Mrs Mapp-Flint to see you. She pushed she way into the hall would you believe!"

Irene did find it hard to believe as Lucy tended to dissuade anyone from entering unannounced. 'Must be urgent', she thought.

"Ah, Quaint one at last," Elizabeth said as she appeared round the door. "I'm glad I've caught you, I need a favour, dear Irene."

"Well Mapp it sounds urgent. I'll help if I can but I'm off to Folkestone again tomorrow. I'm going to try and paint the sea would you believe. It will be a real challenge for me. I've rented a beach house from a friend so as to be right on the front."

"Very interesting. I'm sure you will produce some wonderful creations, but what I came to ask was, could I rent Taormina until the end of August as I've managed to get a tenant for *Grebe.*"

"You did nothing but complain when you stayed here last time. Are you sure you want to return? I won't have time to clean up but if you look after it for me while I'm away you can have it cheap."

"Oh Irene! So kind, don't worry Benjy and I will take great care of it, I have always said that you're such a good friend, Irene."

"I don't know about that. You can move in tomorrow if you want."
***

The next day was a very busy one in the Mapp-Flint household. Benjy had strict instructions to keep out of the way while Elizabeth and Withers packed all the necessary clothing and toiletries. Mary was told to clean right through as the Colonel was expected that afternoon and everywhere needed to be spotless. Cook had been dispatched to *Taormina* to ensure that it was at least presentable before they all arrived.

Elizabeth was supervising the packing of the cases into the car when a large Daimler pulled up outside the house and a tall distinguished looking man got out.

"You must be Mrs Mapp-Flint," he said as he walked over "I'm Colonel Shyton pleased to meet you."

"Goodness Colonel I didn't expect you until this afternoon. We still have some cleaning to do before you can move in."

"Oh don't worry Mrs Mapp-Flint I will get my man to finish off, I really want to move in as soon as possible."

Elizabeth noticed, as he swung the boot of his car open that, as well as a large number of suitcases, he appeared to have various items of photographic equipment.

"It looks like you intend to do some photography," she said peering in.

"My Benjy is always saying we should take it up now that the modern cameras are so easy to use, none of that fiddling with light meters or anything."

"Yes, there are some small cameras on the market but I use a more sophisticated model as I have been commissioned to take some pictures for the '*Picture Post*' magazine in their 'Our Town' series. They are covering a number for small towns, including Broadstairs, Banbury and Hexham. They have asked me to photograph Tilling."

"How wonderful, I don't think we've been in a magazine before. Wait till I tell everyone, they'll be thrilled."

"I hope to meet some of the residents as I will need to know the best features of the town. I must pick your brains Mrs Mapp-Flint as to who I should see."

"Yes, I'm very influential in the town I've been on the town council and I'm a member of the hanging committee."

"Oh dear, I hope you won't hang me!"

"Oh, no it's for the art exhibition next month." she said with a laugh.

"It sound wonderful. I shall look forward to it. Well I must get on if you've no objection, I'll get my man to move my things into the house at once. If you could just show me round."

Elizabeth hurried ahead leading him into the house as she said, "it's one of the finest houses in the area you know."


Major Benjy had been dozing in the garden all morning and the arrival of the car had woken him up. He thought he'd better see who it was and if he was needed. As he appeared round the side of the house he saw Elizabeth and the Colonel coming out of the front door.

"Well, old girl, what have you been up to in there?"

"Don't be silly Benjy. This is Colonel Shyton who's taking the house for the summer."

"Sorry old chap. No offence meant, just my little joke."

"Go and help Withers finish loading the car," she said pushing him up the path, "So sorry about that we've had a busy morning. Anyway, as to the people you should see I would recommend Mr and Mrs Wyse, very nice people and they've lived in the town for many years. Diva Plaistow would also be helpful. Nothing much she misses. I wouldn't bother with Mr and Mrs Quantock they've only been in the town a few months and would be useless. As for Lucia and Georgie they give the impression of knowing everything but it's all bluff you know. Such a dear couple but they are not original Tillingites. Anyway, that should be enough to go on with. Any problems, make sure you come to and see me I'm well known for sorting things out in Tilling, I'll leave you my new address."

"Well thank you Mrs Mapp-Flint I will certainly take your advice." Elizabeth left the colonel and joined Benjy in their car and drove round to Quaint Irene's. When they arrived, Cook was busy in the kitchen making huffing and puffing noises.

"A fine mess!" she said as Elizabeth appeared.

"Oh dear. Well do your best. I must go into town. I've important business to attend to. Benjy sort the luggage out for me."

"Whatever you say old girl."

As she walked down the High Street she met Lucia coming out of the newsagent's. "Any news, Elizabeth?" She said holding the local paper.

"Yes, my new tenant has arrived. A very nice man a photographer for *The Picture Post*. Said he'd be too busy to spend time with anyone though. Such a shame! I'm sure he would have enjoyed one of your little musical evenings."

"He soon arrived. What's his name?"

"Colonel Shyton from London. Most obliging as well."

"If he's the Shyton I know, he's a terrible man stays in bed all day. His poor ex-wife, Babs, was so long suffering during their divorce. I met her when I stayed in London before the war."

"It can't be the same person. He looked quite active and said he would be busy all the time with his photography. You don't know everyone Lucia."

"We shall see. It's not a common name. Anyway, enough of this I have to tell you as a member of the hanging committee that the art exhibition this year is cancelled - decorating the hall according to The Mayor, it's here in the local paper."

"What, why didn't he tell me? I'm the senior member of the committee after all."

"I don't know Elizabeth but there you are you know now."

"Anyway, it doesn't matter I won't be doing any painting this year, I've decided to get Benjy's camera out and take some pictures instead. The Colonel might think they're good enough for the magazine you know."

"Well Elizabeth best of luck with that. Must get on."

Lucia had heard enough. She had intended to go to the church to see if the Padre had any ideas about where to hold the art exhibition, but as she walked along, she began to think about what Elizabeth said about taking pictures for a magazine. 'It might be an alternative to the art exhibition if we held a photographic competition instead', she thought. 'Photos are small so we could hold the event at *Mallards*'. She did remember the Colonel from London but hadn't actually met him. She'd felt sorry for his poor wife, Babs, who he divorced over an affair he said she'd had with some Lord or other. Lucia sympathised with her at the time as she denied the whole thing as seemed very genuine. If she were to arrange this photographic competition, she would need to get on his good side so she hoped he would have forgotten her involvement with Babs or even hadn't been aware of it at the time. If she kept quiet she might be able to work things out in her favour.

\*\*\*

The next day was a Sunday, so Diva was able to rest as the tea room was closed until Wednesday. She had put on her best hat and coat and although short and rather portly, she could look quite smart when she tried. She was just about to leave for the church when there was a knock on the door. Upon opening it she was surprised to see a stranger holding a camera.

"Mrs Plaistow, I'm Colonel Shyton. I'm so glad I caught you, I was just passing and thought I'd make myself known"

"Very nice to meet you. Elisabeth's already told me about you. I can't stop I'm afraid I'm just off to church."

"Sorry to interrupt but I wanted to pick your brains. Mrs Mapp-Flint said you would be the best person to ask, as you know everything there is to know about Tilling."

"Did she indeed! I'm sure she meant well. I'm not an expert really you know."

"Well perhaps I could walk to the church with you. I'm not looking for an expert just someone who knows the town."

Diva observed that he was an attractive man for his age, smartly dressed in a grey three-piece suit and trilby. She said she would be delighted. As they walked she outlined some of the main places he may want to photograph and asked him about his project.

"I've been commissioned by *The Picture Post* to take some photos for their magazine but if anyone has any flair in this area I could look at their work and see if it was suitable for publication as well."

"Oh really, how exciting! I've done a little photography in my time I might see what I can do."

The truth was that she'd had a go at taking some pictures a few years ago but could never get the lighting or the focus right and gave it up.

"That would be good, I shall insist on taking you under my wing, so to speak, and guiding you along if you should so need." He finished with a little bow. As they reached the church he made an excuse and said he would call again on Monday if that was convenient.

Diva fairly bounced into church. Lucia was standing in the porch craning to see who she'd been talking to.

"Was that the Colonel who's taken Mapp's house?" she asked.

"Yes, such a nice man! He's going to help me with my photography."

"Really that was quick, even for you Diva. I didn't know you were interested in photography. You'll have to submit something to my little exhibition in August."

"What exhibition? Who's arranged that?"

"I have, there will be no Art Exhibition in the town hall this year and as a member of the hanging committee I have decided to hold a little photographic exhibition at *Mallards.*"

"I'm not sure Mapp will be pleased about that. Have you asked her?"

"No, but she could hardly hold it at Quaint Irene's could she?"

Lucia decided that her next job was to get the Colonel involved. "I'm too busy to go to church today tell Georgie I'll see him later." With that she rushed off in the direction the Colonel had taken. Hurrying along she thought she'd lost him but, as she rounded a corner, she found him setting up his camera tripod by the side of the road.

"Such a nice view from here," she said as she drew level. "I've been hearing all about you from Diva."

"Delighted to meet you. I'm Colonel Shyton." he said looking round.

"Yes I know, Lucia Pillson." She said extending her hand.

"Do you know, you seem familiar, have you ever lived in London?"

"Once very briefly, I'm sure we've never met though."

"I must be mistaken. I had a difficult time in London a while ago. Do you have an interest in photography at all?"

Lucia realised that this was her chance "As a matter of fact I do. This is quite a coincidence as I'm holding a photographic exhibition towards the end of August. Perhaps you could come if you're' still in Tilling."

"I'd be delighted to, I have some experience of such things. I chair a photographic committee in London. Does yours have a theme?"

"Yes, we thought we would make it relevant to the town and its people." She had to think quickly if her plan was to work. "Diva was full of praise about your expertise. I wondered if you would perhaps judge the entrants for us?"

"I can do better than that. *The Picture Post* is hoping to do a series called 'Our Town', so if any photos are good enough I could recommend that they publish them."

"How wonderful, that will certainly get people interested. I'll leave you to get on now as I need to advertise our project as soon as possible."

\*\*\*

Over the next week, Tilling became a hive of activity. A visitor to the town would be unable to walk round without meeting someone photographing something. The Church and the Town Hall had never been photographed so much and even the High Street received its share of photographers. Mr Twistevant was heard complaining to Dodo at the sweet shop about the nuisance of it all.

"Everyone's out with their cameras but no one's coming into the shop to buy anything, I've had the shop front photographed at least a dozen times today already."

"I know, Mr Twistevant, but you have to admit it's a grand idea. I'm off to photograph the church myself when I close up."

At 3.00pm Diva left her tea house on the arm of Colonel Shyton. This had become a daily ritual. The Colonel would arrive at about 1.00pm, take some lunch, free of charge ("I can't make you pay when you have been so helpful") and then they would set off around the town with their cameras to select a spot to photograph. Diva and the Colonel had been 'getting on' rather well. In addition to their afternoon trips the Colonel had visited Diva in the evenings a few times for dinner. She found him very good company and he showed such interest in her life, enquiring about her business.

"You have a little goldmine here Diva, if I may call you Diva?" he said on their first evening together.

"Yes of course you may."

"I expect once the effects of the war are over and rationing ends, you will branch out a little?"

"I had thought I'd open more often and perhaps start to do dinners, but at the moment with the shortages I'm not able to." He said very little about himself, just that he was divorced and worked freelance for various magazines. She didn't like to pry in case he thought her nosey.

A week later they were just about to set up near the town walls when Elizabeth appeared with her camera.

"What a nice surprise," she said, although she'd been in wait for some time. "You can give me some advice about things like angle, perspective and lighting." She had clearly been reading up on the subject.

"Of course Mrs Mapp-Flint. Have you decided on your subject though? You really need to select something first and then I can give you some help with the areas you mention." Before she could continue, Georgie came hurrying round the corner

"I was hoping to bump into you Colonel Shyton," he said. Like Elizabeth, he'd been watching the tea house for a few days to see what time they left so he could catch them.

"Are you looking for help with your perspective as well?" snapped Diva

"Oh, sorry I forgot in my excitement to introduce myself, Mr Pillson. I believe you met my wife, Lucia the other day Colonel."

"I did indeed. A charming lady. Well it looks as though there are several people who need help so why don't we arrange a little meeting to answer any questions you may have?"

"Good idea," said Diva "let's hold it at the tea rooms on Sunday at two. Now if we can get on…"

"So sorry to interrupt your session, dear Diva," said Elizabeth. "See you on Sunday. Come along Georgie, let's leave them in peace, au reservoir."

\*\*\*

Lucia had also seen Diva and the Colonel together several times and she'd noticed how close they were getting. She was very suspicious of him, all this enthusiastic rushing about with a camera, not a bit like people described him in London. As she remembered he was said to be very lazy, staying bed all day, not working at anything and generally unpleasant. She decided to call Stephen Merriall, a friend she had made in London, who usually knew all the gossip. He wrote a column for a London paper under the name of 'Hermione'. He would be sure to know what was going on she thought. Quickly finding his number in her diary she gave him a call at work. Luckily he answered the phone himself.

"Lucia, a long time since we spoke, I still intend to visit you in, where is it? Tilton?"

"Never mind that Stephen, I'm ringing about Colonel Shyton. He's turned up here and is quite the man about town, not at all as I thought he'd be. You said he was old but I would say he's only around 50 something and lively, not lounging in bed all day."

"Well you do surprise me. You're right I think he's 50ish. We just called him old. I know he's been having money troubles. Some shares had become worthless I think and he's moving out of his apartment in Central London and into a smaller place in Chiswick somewhere."

"He's rushing around here with a camera. Said it was to take some pictures for *The Picture Post*"

"I don't know what all that's about. I'll see what I can find out and let you know. How's lovely Georgie? Give him my regards."

"I will, thanks for your help Stephen." As she put the phone down, Georgie came down stairs, carrying his camera as usual.

"I found a book in the town library about someone called, Charles Dodgson but he seems to photograph people, mainly children. Tar'some! Not a bit helpful, still I'm going to a session with the Colonel on Sunday he's agreed to show us the best way to take pictures."

"Very nice, Georgie I've just been speaking to Stephen Merriall about the Colonel."

"Oh him! I could never get on with him too prissy for me."

"Georgie listen, he said that the Colonel is bankrupt and is moving into a smaller apartment."

"Oh poor man, perhaps this job with the magazine will help him."

"No Georgie you're not listening, I'm worried about the way he's getting friendly with Diva. She's doing well at the tea rooms and I'm frightened he's after her money."

"Oh Lucia, I'm sure you're wrong, he seems too nice and is being very helpful with the photography and everything."

"We shall see? Stephen's going to ring me back if he finds anything else out."
\*\*\*

Sunday afternoon and quite a large group had arrived at Diva's house for the photography class. Colonel Shyton ran through the basics with them and tried to demonstrate how to use a light meter and the various camera settings.

"Much depends on the particular camera but, if you have any problems, you can always find me at *Grebe*."

"Really, I tried to catch you twice this week but your man said you were out and he didn't know when you would be back," said Daisy, who'd become rather lost during the talk. She did notice that the Colonel, who sat next to Diva, touched her hand at one point and she saw that Diva didn't pull away but smiled at him.

After the talk, as people were beginning to sit and chat, Georgie took the opportunity to show the Colonel his camera. "It's supposed to be simple but I'm not sure what all these knobs are for?"

"I hope you've settled into *Grebe* aright," said Elizabeth pushing between them "Let me know if there's anything you need."

"Elizabeth, I'm sure you've left him well provided for," interrupted Diva standing up. "Now if we've finished, I need to get on so I must throw you all out."

As they left, Daisy saw that the Colonel didn't appear to be leaving with them and she spotted Diva looking up and down the street before shutting the front door with a loud bang.

Lucia was coming towards them as they turned the corner.

"Have I missed the talk Georgie?"

"Yes Lucia, you're much too late."

"Lucia, have you noticed how close he's getting to Diva?" Said Daisy. "He held her hand today and she didn't pull away."

"Yes, I'm a little concerned about it. I found out that he's impoverished and I'm worried he may have noticed Diva isn't that badly off."

"Lucia don't be silly! I'm sure you're worrying over nothing," said Elizabeth. "He seems perfectly nice to me."

"Well I'm going to keep my eye on him. I may have a word with Diva about him if I find anything out."

\*\*\*

The day of the photographic competition had arrived and Lucia was busy sorting out the sets of pictures that had already come. She'd decided to erect a marquee in the garden as the event had turned out to be so popular. Cadman and Mellors from the golf club, had agreed to help by putting tables from the house along the sides of the tent wall and Lucia was arranging the photos on these with the photographer's name beside each. She had almost finished one side of the marquee when Elizabeth rushed in.

"Why did no one tell me we'd started? As the senior member of the hanging committee I need to supervise all the exhibits."

"Dear Elizabeth, so enthusiastic! I thought you resigned," Lucia replied. "Anyway, there's no hanging to be done. We are just spreading the photos out on these tables as they will be easier to look through."

"Even so I should have been informed. I've brought my little efforts, just a modest set which need to go somewhere prominent otherwise they may be overlooked," she said, pulling a large envelope out of her bag.

"You must have a hundred pictures there Elizabeth I would hardly call it modest."

Lucia watched as she started to set them out on a nearby table, discarding a few and putting them back into the envelope.

"I feel I may have too many of the church. Which do you think are the best?" she asked as she placed a row of photos along the length of the table.

"They all look the same to me. Here just put these two out and pop the rest back into your bag," said Lucia without really looking at them. At that moment, Diva arrived on the arm of Colonel Shyton.

"Where do you want these Lucia? They're mine and the Colonel's."

Lucia took a quick look at the small set of prints she handed her. She was impressed, it was clear Diva had received good advice and the picture of the High Street with her Tea-House in the centre was particularly striking. "They're very good Diva. Let's put them at the front, here," she said pushing some of Elizabeth's pictures aside.

Georgie arrived with the Wyses, who had just returned from Italy and looked very smart with their loose Italian cloths and striking suntans. "Hope you've left room for us?"

"We've taken some lovely views of Tuscany," said Susan. "Shall we put them here?" She pointed to a nearby table.

"Yes of course Susan, but really the theme is Tilling you know. Oh well, they are so nice, I'm sure it won't matter."

Suddenly, everyone seemed to arrive at once and Elizabeth took over setting out the photos by pushing in front of Lucia and taking them as people came through the door. The last person to arrive was Major Benjy holding two rather large views of the Golf course and one of the King's Arms which he spread out on the first table he came to, covering most of the other photos in the process.

As the afternoon progressed, people moved round looking at the pictures and everyone showed great interest, discussing things like lighting and perspective as though they'd been doing it for years. After about an hour, Lucia asked the Colonel to start the judging. At that moment, Grosvenor beckoned her over to tell her she had a phone call.

"Lucia, its Stephen somebody from London." Lucia hurried into the house. "Oh, hallo Stephen, you just caught me in the middle of the photo competition."

"I'm pleased I have. I've found out a bit more about Colonel Shyton and he has been asked by *Picture Post* to visit Tilling regarding the 'Our Town' articles. A friend of mine at the magazine said they were only expecting him to be there, at the most, a week. He is supposed to get the residents to submit their photos to the magazine and they'll pay ten pounds for every one they publish. He said they would only need four or five though."

"Well that's odd because I got the impression he was supplying the photos and would only submit one or two from us."

"Yes, but don't forget he's hard up and if he can submit say four of his own that's forty pounds he's made. Keep an eye on him Lucia I sure he's up to something."

On returning to the marquee she found that the Colonel had whittled the winners down to three sets.

"I am ready to announce the winner," he shouted. Silence fell on the crowd.

"I have two sets that are 'highly recommended' they are Mr and Mrs Wyse's views of Tuscany, most beautiful and a clear sense of frame and atmosphere. The second set are by Mrs Pillson who has taken some very nice pictures; the one she calls *'Mallards at sunset'* is particularly good. But the winner with her pictures of the cobbled streets of Tilling and an outstanding view of the High Street, is Diva Plaistow."

"Oh I'm shocked!" Diva said looking unusually flustered "It's really down to the Colonel as, without his help, I would never have been able to do it."

"I'm also happy to tell you," shouted the colonel over the chatter, "I will be recommending that *The Picture Post* published at least one of her lovely pictures in the next issue." The Colonel then gave Diva, what Lucia thought, was a rather prolonged peck on the cheek. "More like a kiss really," she said to Georgie later.

"Refreshment are available in the house." Grosvenor announced as people began to drift away. Lucia managed to stop Diva just as she was leaving. "A quick word Diva, quite important really."

"Oh dear whatever is it?"

"Diva dear, I tell you this with your welfare in mind as a close friend. I have been speaking to Stephen Merriall in London about the Colonel and what he tells me is a little worrying"

"Lucia, I don't want to hear a lot of gossip! That Stephen is a gossip columnist as I remember."

"It's up to you Diva but you should know that the Colonel is penniless and not only that, he is supposed to recommend *our* photos for the magazine not his own. You must decide for yourself but do take care not to be tricked by him."

"Thank you Lucia, I can look after myself you know, I'm not a complete fool."


Diva was thinking about what Lucia had said all the next day as she set the tables in her tea-house. She'd come to like the Colonel (she still called him Colonel even though he'd told her to call him Bruce). Even so, she was a little concerned about his interest in her business but she felt she could deal with him if he asked her for money. She was expecting to see him in an hour as he phoned earlier to say he had something important to say before he returned to London. After Lucia had told her of his financial state she began to worry about what the important thing was. At 4.00pm, just as the tea-house was closing, he appeared at the door.

"Janet, are you alright to clear up I have to see the Colonel before he goes back to London."

"Yes of course," said Janet, collecting plates.

"Come through Colonel."

When they were settled together in the parlour, what he said came as a complete surprise.

"My dear we have become close and I have come to like you very much so I wanted to….."

Before he could finish she took a deep breath and stood up.

"No don't say anything yet. I want to ask you if you feel the same and if so what you think we should do about it?"

Diva remained standing and had to think quickly. She liked the Colonel but she had to consider what she really wanted. If they what he wanted was marriage she knew that it would be companionship for her. She had felt lonely ever since her beloved dog Paddy died. The Colonel was younger than her, he would be there should she needed support as she got older. On the other hand, she wasn't sure of his motives. She had become settled in her ways and didn't really want to change. Did she want a husband at this stage in her life? Asking herself this brought her to a decision.

"Colonel, I do like you but I don't feel I want a relationship at my age. I'm happy as I am, a little set in my ways and many would say, difficult to get on with. So, I'm sorry Colonel, I don't think we should marry, if that's what you are proposing."

"I can't say I'm not disappointed. You're sure there are no other reasons why you're refusing me. I fear people may have been spreading gossip about me."

"No Colonel I don't listen to gossip, I just don't want to get involved. I've been very flattered by your attention. I know I'm no film star and I never expected anything like this to happen. I do hope you don't feel I led you on. Let's just leave things as they are. I hope you have a safe journey home and thank you for all your help over the past few weeks."

As she spoke, his demeanour began to change and he started to look quite angry. "If that's your last word, there's no more to be said," and with that he stood up and walked out of the room.

Lucia was walking up the High Street, intending to visit Diva and nearly bumped into him as he left the tea house. He didn't speak but pushed past her, jumped into his car and drove away.

On entering the tea-house, Janet told her that Diva was in the back parlour. As she passed through Lucia thought she could hear crying.

"Are you alright Diva darling?" She said on entering the room, "has he said something to upset you? He nearly knocked me over a moment ago."

"No, I'm fine really. It's just the thought of what might have been had I been younger. Oh well I'm a silly old fool to get so upset."

"We have known each other for some years now," Lucia said taking Diva's hand "and we've had our disagreements. But, in the end, we're friends and you have many friends in Tilling. That's the most important thing don't forget."

\*\*\*

A week had gone by and no one had heard anything more from the Colonel and Lucia was keen to know which photos would appear in the magazine. The next issue was due out today and the newsagent had ordered extra copies in view of the interest that it had aroused.

"I don't suppose we'll see any of our pictures in the magazine" said Georgie, as he and Lucia walked to the newsagent.

"You never know Georgino. You could be surprised."

"Oh Lucia, that's just you being optimistic as usual."

As they rounded the corner they saw a large crowd outside the newsagent's shop. A few people were coming out with the magazine, and amongst them were Diva and Quaint Irene, just returned from Folkestone.

"All this fuss about a few photos," said Irene, as they crossed over to Lucia and Georgie. "Now if it had been about something really talented like paintings, it would be worth queuing up."

"Have you got a copy there?" Georgie asked

"Yes have a look." Diva thrust the magazine at Lucia, who saw at once that the front cover was taken up with her own photo of the town from the nearby fields.

"Well that's one of yours, Lucia, look inside." said Georgie leaning over.

Lucia turned to the middle pages where there were three further pictures. One was Diva's view of the High Street with 'Ye Olde Tea-House' in the centre. There was another by Lucia of *Mallards* and a third one of the Church which looked rather like one of Elizabeth's efforts.

"Well, what a surprise, nothing by the Colonel!" Observed Georgie "I wonder how they got all these pictures? I'm sure the Colonel didn't take them when he left."

"No he didn't," said Lucia "I sent them to the magazine. After the show, I collected a few of the better prints and negatives and sent them off on the chance they might publish a few. Looks like it was a good idea."

Later, as Diva sat quietly in her parlour, she looked again at the pictures in the magazine.

"Such a nice spread," she thought to herself "but I'm beginning to feel a little sorry for the Colonel now - no money from the magazine and no money from me either. Oh well that's life!"

The end

## Georgie and the Missing Ring

1.

Georgie was enjoying a few days on his own as Lucia had gone to London to visit her friends in the capital. He had begun to find these visits rather tedious as Lucia reigned supreme, organising everything, arranging where to go and who to visit. Georgie felt as though he had little say in the whole thing. It was always Marcia this or Olga that, he got really fed up with not being the centre of attention. When Lucia said she'd planned to go down for a few days, Georgie immediately made an excuse, saying he felt a little under the weather and would like a quiet time at home. As a result he'd spent the last few days doing whatever he fancied, painting, embordering and shopping; his three favourite activities.

But now it was Friday and Lucia was expected back tonight so Georgie thought he should make the most of his last free day and had decided to cycle somewhere. Cycling wasn't his most popular means of transport but Lucia had taken the car, as usual, now she was able to drive herself about.

"It gives one so much more freedom, you know." She informed him as she packed enough luggage in the boot to last, in Georgie's opinion, as least two weeks rather than three days. Cycling it had to be. Cadman had taught Lucia to ride so Georgie got him to teach the basics such as how to balance on the contraption. After a few bruising falls he managed to get the hang of it. Once he got going he quite enjoyed the whole experience and, although infrequent, he did cycle through the town on occasions especially when he wanted to show off a new outfit.

Today he'd decided to wear his plus-fours for the first time. He'd sent away to Scotland for them and was pleased with the bright pattern off yellow and blue with a dark red over check. Just the right look for cycling, he felt. Hats and cloaks were out of the question so he wore a small cap, the same pattern as the trousers and a tweed jacket of muted colours. He didn't want to look too garish.

"Just enough to get noticed but not to be startling." He decided.

Looking at himself in the hall mirror he was pleased with the effect but still felt there was something was missing. "Perhaps a broch to set off the dark colours of the jacket," he thought. He returned to his room to see what he could find. The task was harder then he thought as none of his collection of jewellery seemed to be right. He held one broch after another up against his coat but none seemed quite right. With a sigh he threw everything back into the jewellery box and slammed the lid. He had a sudden idea; as Lucia was away thought he would sneak into her bedroom and see if she had anything that might look better. As long as he returned it by teatime she would never know.

Georgie rarely visited Lucia's bedroom, in fact he couldn't remember the last time he'd done so.

"Two Christmases ago, on boxing day," he thought "when she said she was feeling *under the weather*," he remembered putting his head round the door to see how she was, but definitely not going into the room.

"Too much sherry on Christmas day," he remembered thinking at the time.


Lucia's bedroom was very tidy, no clothing strew about or half used cosmetics on show, unlike his own room. He knew that Lucia kept her valuable jewellery in a small safe behind a picture on the wall but hoped there would be some less valuable bits in the dressing table. He hunted through the dressing table and bedside cabinet but found nothing he like. A few paste items of dubious quality and some ear rings, all in need throwing away as far as he could see. In desperation he had a quick look at the safe and  to his surprise when he pulled the handle it opened quite easily.

"She must have forgotten to lock it properly." Georgie thought as he lifted a padded box down. Setting it on the bed he carefully opened it to find it contained a lovely set of matching items; broch, necklaces and a large ring with a big red stone. He had a feeling he'd seen Lucia wearing the set on special occasions. Holding the broch up to himself in the mirror, he knew it would look just right on his jacket. It was star shaped with a red stone in the centre to match the ring. Pinning it on he was very pleased with the effect.

"I'll take great care of it and get back by four, well in time to return it to the safe," he thought.

Just as he was about to shut the box he took another look at the ring and decided to wear that as well. "Too nice to leave, they do need to be worn together," he decided, "I will leave the necklace, don't want to overdo it."

After he'd slipped the ring onto his right index finger he left the box on the bed and hurried downstairs.

2

It was a lovely spring day and Georgie was enjoying cycling through the town. He hadn't gone far when he spotted Elizabeth Mapp-Flint coming out of the wool shop. Elizabeth had hoped to sneak into shop early so as not to be seen. She had heard that here was to be a knitting competition in a few weeks organised by Daisy Quantock . The idea was that after the event the knitwear would be donated to the poor in the parish. Elizabeth had heard that the local press would be present at the prize giving and then the winner of the best item would present all the knitwear to the Salvation Army. Elizabeth was keen to get involved and have her picture in the local paper holding, what she hoped would be the winning jumper. She had a vision of herself handing the knitwear over to the Salvation Army while the cameras flashed. She knew she was a little rusty having done no knitting for some time but decided it was something easily picked up again. In the event of a disaster she had already hunted out a couple of Benjie's old jumpers that he'd hardly worn and would present them as her own work but hoped it wouldn't be necessary.

"Good morning Elizabeth, going to do some knitting?" He called.

"Yes Georgie," she said as she folded a knitting pattern and stuffed it into her bag. "Must keep busy you know."

"Are you going to enter the competition then?"

"Well I'll have to see; my little efforts may not be good enough but one must support good causes. What about you? Can you knit as well as embroider?"

"I'm better at crochet but I'll give it a try. Lucia said she would help me."

"You look smart are you off somewhere nice? What a nice broch and that ring, it must have cost a lot, present from dear Lucia no doubt; so generous."

"Um yes lovely. Well I'm off on a short ride as the weather is so nice and Lucia's in London."

"Yes I heard such a busy soul. Well can't stop and chat must get on, Au reservoir," with that she hurried down the road.

Georgie was just about to mount his bike again when Quaint Irene appeared round the corner holding a satchel.

"My what a sight you are, all dressed up, where did you get that lovely broch?" She asked pulling at his lapel.

"Oh it's nothing just some costume jewellery to set off the jacket. What are you doing?"

"Don't ask! I've been pressurised by Daisy to bake a cake for this retched knitting hoo-ha. I hate baking I don't know why I agreed. Wouldn't like to take over would you?"

"No! I've no idea how you bake cakes."

"Well you can help now as I've got to nip to the shop. I've no vanilla essence and I need more milk. The recipe Daisy gave me includes all sort of stuff I had to buy specially. Would you look after the studio for a minute while I rush off? I'm on my own today."


Georgie really wanted to get on but agreed to stand by the door while she was away, what she though anyone would want to seal was beyond him. When he looked inside, the place was a mess with paints and brushes scattered about everywhere. There was a large easel set up at one end with a brightly coloured half finish painting on it. Georgie walked over but even at close range, was unable to tell what it was supposed to be. On the table in the middle of the room was a large bowl with two half empty bags of flour, some egg shells and a bowl of sugar. A wooden spoon was sticking out of the bowl which, Georgie saw, contained a lumpy milky mixture with a few raisins floating in it.

"What a mess!" He thought taking hold of the spoon. "I'll see if I can sort it out a bit."

He grasped the spoon with both hands and started to stir the mixture round. It was quite thick and difficult to managed but once he got it moving it became easier and he began to get into the swing of it.

"Get hold of this Georgie." Said Irene who had come up behind him and handed him a bottle of milk, "poor some in I think it might need a bit more. I followed the receipt but it didn't say what to do if it went lumpy."

Georgie caught hold of the milk as he continued to stir with his right hand.

"It's getting better I think, you'll have to keep stirring it."

"Oh leave it I'll sort it out." Irene said as she took the spoon from him and nudged him aside, "Oops, I think something's fallen into the bowl. Oh dear it's a flake of plaster from the ceiling, see there I'll scoop it out."

"Irene! That's no good, have any more bits fall in?"
"No, don't worry Georgie it'll all mix together, it's only old whitewash."

"Well I won't be eating any, that's for sure. Look I must get off. All the best with the cake." With that he struggled back onto his bike and rode, rather wobbly, away.


Georgie enjoyed a pleasant day on his own. He did a few quick sketches of the country-side while sitting in the sun feeling dozy. When he looked at his watch he was surprised to see it was nearly three o'clock and Lucia would be back at four. He jumped up packed his sketch book in the saddle bag and peddled quickly to Mallards to replace the broch before she got back.

He arrived just before four and was relieved to see that Lucia's car wasn't in the drive. Running up to the bedroom he quickly unpinned the broch and placed it carefully back in the box. He was just about to put it in the safe when he remembered the ring but, to his horror, it was no longer on his finger. He hunted round the bedroom floor to no avail and remembered that Elizabeth has remarked on it when he met her in town so he must have had it at that time. He wracked his brains trying to think where he might have lost it. He'd been up to the golf club and round past Grebe so it could have been anywhere. He decided that all he could do would be to ride round again and see if he could see it on the roadside. He dare not tell Lucia it was missing, she'd go mad. He was sure it was a favourite set as he remembered seeing her wear it only on special occasions. He put the box back in the safe and closed the door. He had to turn the dial so that Lucia would think it had been locked all the time. If he found the ring he would have to find a way of getting it back to her without raising suspicion.

Lucia had enjoyed her visit to friends in London and caught up on all the gossip but she was glad to be home. Parking her car she called for Grosvenor. As soon as she got in.

"Yes madam?"

"Would you please run me a bath I'm absolutely exhausted. Where's Georgie, in his room?"
"No madam I've not seen him all day he went out on his bike this morning and as far as I know he's not back yet. I did think I heard him moving about not long ago but the bike's not in the garage so he must

still be out."

"How odd, he hates that bike, only stays on it about an hour at a time. Oh well let me know when he gets back and we'll have some tea."


Georgie did hate the bike and as he peddled round he was hating it more and more, He dare not go too fast in case he missed ring but the further he peddled the less likely he thought he'd find it and what was worst it was beginning to get dark as he turned, exhausted, back home.

3

When Lucia came down for breakfast she noticed that Georgie had already eaten.

"Has Georgie gone back to bed?" She asked as Grosvenor walked in with her boiled egg on a tray.

"No madam he went out straight after breakfast."
"How odd, I feel as though he's avoiding me. He hardly said anything at teatime yesterday, just how tired he was and went to bed early. I didn't have a chance to tell him about my London trip. I do hope he's alright."


In fact Georgie was not 'alright'. He'd decided it was useless running round looking for the ring so he thought he'd try asking people in the town whether they'd found it. This he knew had to be carried out with care so as not to arouse suspicion. The last thing he wanted was people asking Lucia if she'd found her ring. He'd no sooner reached the High Street when he bumped into Diva coming out of Twistevant's.

"Hallo Georgie you're up early, did Lucia get back from London OK?"
"Yes, she's fine, have you been far?"
"Far? No just the usual shopping. I have to start early to be ready to open

the teashop, why?"

"Oh no reason I just wondered if anything had happened while you walked round, you know did you **find** anything?"

"Find anything? I don't know what you mean, of course didn't find anything. Did you?"

"No, no it's just um I heard that Dodo from the sweet shop lost her…um.. cat you know."

"Did she? She never said anything when I went in. I didn't know she had a cat."

"Yes um.. I think it was her that lost a cat, I'm not sure now. Anyway you've not seen it then?"

"No, no cats at all." With that she hurried away looking puzzled and glancing back at Georgie as she turned the corner.

"Well that was a disaster, I'll have to think of something better than that." Georgie thought to himself.

As it was early there were few people about so he decided to visit the Wyses. Just to pop in to wish them good morning and see if they'd found anything.

Susan opened to door to his knock, "Georgie! What a surprise we were just going out. Algernon! Georgie's here."

"Oh sorry to disturb you. I was just passing and thought I'd see how you were."

"We're both fine, about to drive into town can we give you a lift?"

This was all rather silly as Georgie had just walked from the town and it had taken him about five minutes in all.

"No, I'd prefer to walk. Have you been out today yet, I wondered if you'd come across anything exciting?"

"Exciting in Tilling! Algernon did go for a short walk, didn't you dear? She asked him as he appeared in the doorway. "Georgie was asking if you came across anything exciting when you were out."

"No Georgie, nothing to mention, I did spot Padre hurrying to church and almost bumped into the postman, other than that it was very dull. Nothing exciting I'm afraid." He replied with a laugh.

"That's Tilling for you." Georgie said backing out of the way as the Wyses bundled into their car. "Have a nice trip."

Georgie watched as they drove away feeling even more embarrassed.

"I'll have to stop all this, it's not working." He thought to himself "I'll just have to come clean to Lucia that's all. I'll leave it a few days in case the ring turns up."


In fact Georgie left it completely, as Lucia said nothing about the ring, he hoped she'd forgotten she ever had one. It was the day before the knitting competition and Lucia had made a rather nice bonnet. She'd varied the colours as she went along using up bits of left over wool and had cleverly knitted a set of pretty flowers which she sewed round the rim.

"Lucia that's' lovely." Georgie said when she tried it on that morning, "I wish I could knit as good."

George had managed to produce a short scarf. He'd tried to crochet something but decided it would take too long so Lucia sat with him one night and taught him an easy stich. She'd said that the most difficult part about knitting was remembering to move the yarn back and forth when working through the stich and showed him the way to do it. Georgie was surprised how quickly he'd picked it up and began to enjoy the work sitting with Lucia in the evenings both knitting in the garden room and listening to classical music on the new gramophone.

He produced a scarf, brightly stripped but a little small, just long enough to fold round his neck if he pulled it when he tried it on.

"I'd have like to make it longer but there's not enough time, why Daisy decided on such short notice for the preparation I don't know."
"I think it's something to do with the Salvation Army's schedule anyway we've produced something. When I saw Elizabeth yesterday she was very odd and wouldn't say what she'd done, just that she'd worked hard and hoped her little effort would please."

"Quaint Irene told me that the Wyses had borrowed a knitting machine which seems a bit of a cheat."
"Don't be silly Georgie there's no such thing, it's just Quaint Irene's way of causing trouble, you know what she's like. I heard from Diva that she'd made a lovely cake and given it to Janet to ice so I'm looking forward to trying some at the competition tomorrow."

"Lucia I'd give it a miss I saw what went in it!"

"Don't be silly Georgie I'm sure it'll be delightful. Now, what shall I wear?"
"Oh nothing special it's only in the church hall I'm just going in my yellow and brown jacket with the matching check trousers and cape."
"Well I don't call that nothing special. I'll have to think about it , I'm sure I've got some nice jewellery I've not worn recently, want to stand out a bit don't we?"

No Lucia!" shouted Georgie, "you mustn't wear expensive jewellery, I've heard there are terrible thieves about only last week the Padre's wife had her bag snatched."
"Did she, Evie never said anything when I saw her yesterday I'll have to ask her about it."

"No don't she's too upset and you'll make her cry."

"Don't be silly Georgie she's not going to cry, she may squeak a bit but I can't ever remember her crying."

"Anyway Lucia your pearls will be fine." Georgie said in desperation dreading her opening the safe to find the ring missing.

"I suppose your right, it's not really a special event and it is for charity so one can't look too prosperous I can one."

Georgie breathed a sigh of relief and resolved to tell her the truth after the competition was over.

4

Daisy Quantock was in a fluster. It was the day of the knitting competition and nothing was going right. The Padre had called at breakfast with the news that the hall was double booked and the local darts team were holding a match at the same time as the competition.

"Och, I'm so sorry Mrs Quantock, Evie must have got confused and booked the wrong day. Is there any way you could rearrange your event?"

"No Padre I've everything organised, Diva's Janet is bringing the cake and Diva has sorted out some catering. The Salvation Army people are turning up at noon to play us a tune with their band and the local paper is also coming. I can't cancel everything now."

"I can see the problem, I'll just have to speak to the darts group and see if they could have their competition in the public house after all that's where they usually go."

"Oh thank you Padre that would be good."

"Failing that, as the hall is quite large and there is the stage, we could pull the curtains across and they would then be able to play up there. I'm sure it would work."

"I had hoped to have the winner announced on the stage but I'll see if I can organise something else."


Georgie still hadn't decided what to wear, he'd tried several outfits on but thought he ought to wear something knitted for the competition. All he could find in the bottom of his wardrobe was a rather drab jumper he hadn't worn for some time because it made him look a little fat round the middle. He pulled it on and tucked it in at the back but still it looked very lumpy.

"No good I look like that awful comedian Max someone, no I'll just have to wear this brown and yellow jacket but I'm not happy with it."

When he went down, Lucia was already in the hall. She was wearing a dark red slim fitting dress with matching coat. She held a small red hat which she twisted round and round in a worried way.

"Georgie something terrible has happen!"
"Whatever's the matter you look as though you've lost something."
"I have, my ruby ring! Oh Georgie do you think it's been stolen."
Georgie didn't know what to say for a moment. He took a deep breath and was just about to tell her the truth when Grosvenor appeared.

"Shall I call the police Madam. I've looked everywhere and can't find it."
"No! No police I'm sure it'll turn up," Georgie shouted as he hurried down the stairs.

"It was in my safe and I can't see how it could have been stolen because the safe was locked and only I know the combination."
"Well there you are, as I said It'll turn up, stop worrying. I thought you were wearing your pearls?"

"I was but decided this ruby necklace would go better with the dress and when I opened the box the ring was missing."

"You must have put it somewhere else, we'll have a proper look later, come on or we'll be late for the competition."
"Yes I suppose your right Georgie."

"I've got the knitwear, Madam."

"Thank you Grosvenor we should be back by teatime." She replied taking the parcel.
With that they left the house and started off to the church hall.


When they arrive it looked chaotic to Georgie, with people running round tables carrying bundles of knitting. He spotted Mr Hopkins, the fishmonger, stripped to the waist hauling a large table across the room. There was a rail set up for larger pieces and some hat stands. Daisy was busy directing the chaos. She was shouting instructions to a couple of ladies from the town, telling them where to put items.

"Jumpers on that table Mrs Twistevant! No not there at the end. Look you're dropping everything, take one thing at a time for heaven's sake. Lucia! Thank goodness see if you can sort out the scarves, they're such a tangle, I'll never be able to tell who knitted what."

"Don't fuss Daisy, leave it to me."

Georgie took the two pieces they'd brought and placed them at the end of a nearby table. He was just about to find a seat when Diva came in followed by Janet carrying a large box.

"The cake, Daisy where shall I put it?"
"On the side table near the kitchen please Diva, did you bring any

sandwiches?"

"Yes don't worry it's all arranged. Janet will bring them across later."

Georgie was keen to see the cake and tried to open the lid of the box a little.

"Leave that Georgie I'll see to it later."
"I helped to make it you know, did quite a lot of stirring while Irene went to the shop, helped to get the mixture smooth."
"Yes, I'm sure you did, very kind."

The chaos was coming together and as far as he could see most of the knitwear had arrived. Georgie heard a car door slam outside and Susan Wyse appeared with something wrapped in cellophane.

"Where shall I put this dress?" she asked walking over to Daisy.

"Oh my that's very nice!"

Daisy pulled the covering up to reveal a tightly knitted blue dress, "looks almost shop bought, so skilled of you Susan. Hang it on the rail."

"Must have used a knitting machine." whispered Lucia in Georgie's ear "what a cheat. No Algernon?" she called over.

"No he's coming later with the darts club, where are they to play Daisy"

"Up on the stage, Padre has sorted it all out and pulled the curtains over so they shouldn't be a problem."

"Mr Twistevant won't be happy with that." Said his wife who had overheard the conversation.

"Well there was no alternative the hall had been double booked, I blame Evie, she's such a scatter brain."

Mrs Twistevant was just about to reply when Elizabeth arrived and pushed her aside.

"Daisy darling where shall put my little knitting effort?"

She was holding a large shopping basket.

"What is it Elizabeth? Everything is placed in sections as you can see."
"Oh just a simple jumper, no time to do anything fancy."

With that she pulled a large patterned jumper out of the basket and held it up. There was some sort of zigzag design across the front of the jumper that looked professionally knitted.

"My word that must have taken some doing Elizabeth," remarked Diva feeling the hem.

"Oh it was nothing, must do our bit for charity. Have the press arrived yet?"
"No not yet," replied Daisy "just put it over there with the other jumpers."
Elizabeth crossed over to the table and Georgie noticed she pushed aside most of the other items to clear some room. He went over to have a closer look.

"Well Elizabeth you have been busy, all I could make in the time was a little scarf."
"I'm sure it's delightful dear Georgie so kind."

Georgie turned back the neck of the jumper and noticed that something had been unpicked. He decided to say nothing but was sure the jumper had been bought from a shop.

By noon everyone was assembled and because they were unable to use the stage Padre stood on a couple of boxes that Mr Hopkins had found in the cellar.

"It is so good of you all to come," he started off, "so without further ado, I'm going to ask Mrs Wellford from the Mothers Union to judge the work. Thank you Mrs Wellford do please get started."
Before he could say any more the door burst open and Mr Twistevant march in followed by Major Benjy, Algernon Wyse and Quaint Irene. All were clutching sets of darts and Mr Twistevant held a large dart board.

"This will not do!" he shouted as he came nearer, "we have the Riseholm team coming for this important local match and we can't hold it on a stage and that's final. Padre you will have to sort this out."

Padre looked worried he scratched his head and lent over to whisper with Daisy. After a few nods and shaking of heads he stood up again.

"I'm so sorry you have been inconvenienced Mr Twistevant but we had no choice. The stage is quite large and I've put all the lighting on so I'm sure if you have a look you will find it satisfactory."
"Humph, well we shall see. I will be putting a complaint in at the next trades council meeting. Come along we'll take go and see."
With that the three men climbed onto the stage and disappeared behind the curtain. Quaint Irene, who'd stayed behind, stood next to Lucia.

"Well darling one what a fuss." She said linking her arm.

"Yes Irene I hear you and Georgie made the cake, very unlike you."

"Oh I like to do my bit but Georgie hardly did anything just gave it a stir."

"I may have only given it a stir but I helped to get rid of some of the lumps before you dropped something in it Irene."

"Dropped something in the cake, how awful, what was it? Did you fish it out?"

"It was nothing just a bit of dust. Reluctantly I must leave you, I'll have to practice my darts if we're to beat that Riseholm lot."

She leapt onto the stage and vanished behind the curtain.


After about half an hour, Mrs Wellford came to the end of her deliberations and stood with the Padre on the makeshift podium.

"Are we all ready? Thank you Mrs Wellford."
"You have all done very well," she said "and there are a few outstanding pieces of knitwear. In third place I have chosen this rather nice bonnet with knitted flowers."
"Oh that's mine thank you." Said Lucia looking slightly embarrassed.
"In second place, and it was a close thing, I have decided to put this wonderful knitted coat," she continued as she held up Susan's work.

"How unexpected I never thought it would get a notice." She lied.

"And in first place, because of the intricate work involved, I have chosen this lovely jumper." She concluded and held up Elizabeth's effort.

"Oh no I couldn't accept it, it was nothing surly there are better pieces. No! well I'd just like to say…"
Before she could go any further Benjy appeared from behind the stage curtain and shouted. "What are you doing with my jumper put it down I paid a fortune for it."
"No Benjy it's not the same one!"
"Of course it is I'd recognise it anywhere old girl."

He jumped from the stage and grabbed the jumper from Mrs Wellford.

"Look there's the label."

Sure enough inside, sewn into the bottom edge was a makers label.

"Oh dear how silly of me, I've brought the wrong jumper, this is the original I was copying from."
"Do you want to go home and get your proper jumper, I sure we can wait." Asked Diva with a knowing look at Lucia.
"No, no we should get on, go back to your darts Benjy and I'll take this home don't worry."
Georgie felt a little sorry for Elizabeth as it was clear that no one believed her story of a second jumper. He watched as she put the jumper in her basket and left the hall. Still serves her right, how did she think she'd get away with it, he thought to himself.

"So," announced Padre "Mrs Wyse is the winner well done. Tea is served and The Salvation Army have just arrived to play us a tune."

There was a clattering outside and the doors opened to admit six salvation army people. All dressed in their uniforms they marched round the hall playing 'Onward Christian Solders'. Georgie was really enjoying the show when suddenly the curtains on the stage drew back and Mr Twistevant stepped forward.

"Can we have some quiet please, the other team will be here soon and we will require complete silence so that we can concentrate on the match. Thank you." Pulling back the curtain he disappeared again. The band ground to a halt with an out of tune squawk. Daisy rushed forward, "I'm so sorry for that, please help yourself to sandwiches we'll be cutting the cake soon."


In the meantime the press photographer from the local paper had arrived and began taking pictures of Susan and the Padre handing over the knitwear to the Captain of the Salvation Army. While this was going on the Riseholm darts team arrived, headed by none other than Robert Quantock.

"Robert! You didn't tell me you were coming, what are you doing in that team you should be with the Tilling team now."
"I felt that I still have to be loyal to Riseholm after all I was a member of the team for some years."
Daisy looked a bit unset but didn't say anything as Robert disappeared behind the curtain.

Elizabeth had returned un-notice and was tucking into a plate full of sandwiches.

"Not brought the right jumper back then?" said Diva as she handed her a cup of tea.

"No I feel the moment has passed when people would appreciate my hard work. I shall find a worthy charity to donate it to. What did you knit Diva?" She enquired knowing full well that Diva had never really got the hang of knitting. She'd told everyone she felt it was a waste of time when things were so easily available in the shops. Diva ignored the question and returned to the kitchen.

"Such a martyr, closing her tea shop to provide her delicious sandwiches for us don't you think Georgie?"
"What Elisabeth?" He hadn't really been concentrating as he was watching Janet lifting the cake out of its box. While he'd been standing around he'd thought about the cake mix and wondered how Irene had been able to get rid of the lumps. He remembered what a mess it looked when he was stirring it. In a flash he suddenly recalled the ruby ring being on his finger at the time but not seeing it after that. With a gasp he

thought about Irene saying something had fallen in the mix and panicking he decided he needed to speak to her.

When he got up on the stage he could hear counting going on the other side of the curtain. A voice said, "you'll need double top to draw even." Georgie had no idea what it was all about and he put his head round the curtain as Robert was about to achieve the double. Georgie's actions shook the board which was set at the back of the curtain and with a crash it fell over.

"I say Pillson look what you've done."
"So sorry Major Benjy I just wanted to speak to Quaint Irene."

"Get out you've ruined the set."

Georgie backed away and climbed down to the hall.

"What is it Georgie?" asked Irene as she jumped down beside him.

"Oh Irene I was just wondering if you found anything in the cake mix, you said something dropped into it."
"No Georgie I told you it was just plaster what else could have drop in it."
"Nothing I suppose, it's just that they are cutting it up now."
"Go and bring me a piece and have one yourself. Stop fussing there nothing in the cake"

When Georgie returned to the table he could see that Janet had begun to cut some slices off. She had done a good job of icing, all white with two little figures on the top that looked as though they'd been knitted. Elizabeth was already walking away with a large slice and Lucia had been given a sizable chunk.

"You'll have to help me with this it's much too big." She said breaking it in half.

"Leave it Lucia, perhaps we should get back."
"Don't be silly Georgie It's only two o'clock we've plenty of time yet."

He watched as Lucia bit into her slice, dreading she would find the ring. He hoped he was wrong and it wasn't in the cake at all as he bit into the piece Lucia had given him. A larger piece broke off than he intended but he tried to eat it rather than spit it out. The cake was very sweet and rather solid, if fact the piece Georgie had in his mouth was completely hard. He tried to bite into it without success. Swallowing a small chunk his tongue felt sometime smooth remaining in his mouth and he knew at once what it was.

"Are you having trouble with that Georgie?" Asked Elizabeth as she came over to him. "Try not to choke, better give me your plate and I'll finish it off for you."

Georgie couldn't speak, if he opened his mouth he feared the ring would pop out but he knew he couldn't swallow it. He began to panic.

"Georgie are you aright, you've gone quite red in the face," said Lucia touching his arm.

Georgie nodded and flapped his hands. His only course of action was to get away as quickly as possible.


While this was happening the darts match had come to an end and the players were climbing off the stage. Most had gone to the food stall but Benjy spotted Elizabeth and came over to see what was happening. When he saw Georgie choking he knew what to do at once.

"Stand aside I've done this before. In the Punjab people were always choking."

With that he grabbed Georgie from behind  and pulled him sharply upward. Georgie's mouth opened and something short across the room.

"There you're all tip top." Said Benjy setting Georgie down again.

"Oh thank you Major that was a life saver he was going very red. Are you alright Georgie?"
"Yes, yes I need to lie down."

Lucia led him to a chair beside the door.

"I'll go and see what it was that nearly choked you."
"No Lucia don't leave me, it was just a piece of cake"

Lucia pulled up a chair and sat with him while people looked round to see what had been causing all the trouble. Susan came over and asked if they would like a lift home to which Georgie agreed, anything to get out of the hall before the ring was found.

He said he was feeling better and started to walk towards the door, as he did Irene came up beside him.

"Good job you didn't bring me any cake Georgie she whispered in his ear but you'd better pop this in your pocket I think."

She slipped something into his hand. He knew at once what it was and stuffed it into his pocket.

"Thank you Irene you're an angel."

5

As soon as they arrived home Georgie said he needed to rest and hurried up to his room. He had to find a way of getting the ring back to Lucia without causing suspicion. There was no possibility of returning it to the safe, he'd no idea of the combination and if he tried to go into Lucia's bedroom she might hear and ask what he was doing, No, he had to think of another way. Perhaps it would be best if **she** found it. He could put it somewhere she was likely to look, but the problem was where.

After an hour of deliberation, Georgie decided to go down for tea. First he went to the bathroom and gave the ring a good wash. He didn't want her to find cake stuck to it. Putting it in his pocket he went down stairs to the garden room. Just as he reached the hall he met Grosvenor walking through carrying a tray with the tea things on it.
"Oh Master Georgie I thought you were upstairs I'll get another cup."
"Don't bother Grosvenor I'll get it, you go and see to Lucia."
He thought if he went to the kitchen he might think of somewhere to put the ring but as soon as he entered he knew it was hopeless. Lucia rarely went to the kitchen and when she did it was only to ask Grosvenor something. As he lifted a cup and saucer out of the cupboard he spotted the biscuit barren on the table. Grosvenor must have left it there to take through later. Georgie has a sudden idea, opening the lid he dropped the ring inside.

"She's sure to want a biscuit and will find the ring herself.

When he entered the Garden Room he found Lucia sitting by the fire pouring the tea.

"Oh Georgino mio how are lickle you, feeling better?"
"Yes much better, I've brought the biscuits I know you like them."

"Thank you Georgie, I'll have one later. Oh good you brought another cup, put it down and I'll poor your tea. I thought we'd have it by the fire

as it's getting a little chilly."
"Lovely."

Grosvenor had made some nice egg sandwiches and a set on fairy cakes and they sat in silence listening to the gramophone. Lucia had selected some Chopin that she wanted to learn.

"More tea Georgie," she asked when the record had ended "I do love that piece don't you?"
"Yes but do you think it sound a little difficult to play?"
"Um, you might be right."
Georgie lifted the biscuit barrel. "Do have a biscuit there're your favourites."

In fact he'd no idea what they were as he'd taken no notice when he dropped the ring inside.

"Oh no Georgie I couldn't eat another thing, I really shouldn't have had that second fairy cake."
"I asked Grosvenor get these biscuits specially for you do try one."
"Well as you've gone to so much trouble I'll just have one."
"Choose carefully you don't want a broken one." he said to encourage her to look inside. He hoped the ring hadn't slipped too far down or he'd have to pretend to drop them on the floor or something.

"They look to be all custard creams, I'm not really bothered about them Georgie but thank you for the thought."
Georgie gave the barrel a shake "I think there are some other sorts underneath have a look."
Lucia poked her finger round and Georgie gave the barrel another shake.

"No I won't bother" she said as she withdrew her hand. To Georgie's surprise as her hand came out he saw that the ring had somehow slipped onto her finger.

"Lucia! What's that!"

"Oh my goodness It's my ruby ring, how on earth did it get in there?"

Thinking quickly he said, "it must have fallen in last time you had a biscuit."

"Don't be silly Georgie I've not worn the ring for months and it couldn't have been in the barrel all that time Grosvenor would have notice it."

"She may not have if it was right at the bottom, she would just pile biscuits in over the top."

"I suppose you could be right it's the only explanation. I will have to have a word with her though, she should clean the barrel after each lot of biscuits."

"Lucia stop fussing at least you've found you ring."

"Yes Georgie thank goodness and it's all down to you if you hadn't insisted that I should have a biscuit we may never have found it."


Lucia rang for Grosvenor to clear away and didn't mention the biscuit barrel, just said the ring had come to light.

"I'm so pleased Madam. Miss Irene is waiting in the hall shall I ask her to come in?"

"Of course, you shouldn't have kept her waiting."

Quaint Irene burst into the room at that moment.

"She didn't I was taking my boots off it's coming on to rain. Just popped in the see how the lovely Georgie was after his ordeal."

"I'm fine thank you Irene. Would you like tea, it may be a bit cold by now though."

No won't stop, glad to hear your top-ho. Look after him now Lucia."

"I will and I found my ring."

"Well that's something else to be pleased about. You should take it easy for a few days Georgie. No more dashing about, we don't want anything else getting lost." She said with a wink.

"I certainly will I've decided no more tarsome cycling, no more fiddly knitting and definitely no more cake making."

The end

## Lucia entertains

Georgie had been busy all morning. It was the end of December and he wanted to be ready for Christmas. He would never forget that terrible Christmas when Lucia was swept away in the floods, so now they arrange a dinner each year to celebrate her safe return. Lucia and Georgie refused to join in the annual Christmas card ritual that their friends seemed to enjoy so much. Such a silly and useless thing to do, he always thought and so instead they give everyone a small present.

As Georgie sat at the breakfast table making a list of the people they would invite to the dinner, Lucia came in with the local newspaper.

"Georgino, leave that and look at today's *Echo* they're saying that The Duke of Windsor is coming to Tilling again and intends to stay at Ardingly Park."

"The Duke of Windsor who's he?"

"You of all people should know with your connections Georgie! He used to be Edward the eighth but resigned when he married that American woman."

"Oh him! So he's The Duke of Windsor now. I thought he'd gone abroad."

"He did, some ambassador job but he must be back for Christmas."

"Well I'm not bothered. We had all that fuss last time he came and he tricked us all, can you remember? We went to the station to see him and he slipped in by car unnoticed."

"Yes, but Georgie it's been confirmed this time that he's coming by train. So everyone will be going to the station again. The town will be empty and we can go and get all our Christmas shopping done."

"What a good idea Lucia, I never thought of that."

"We must decide what to get everyone for Christmas, I thought perhaps brooches or tie pins might be a good idea?"

"Yes, but we should have a look around the town and perhaps we can find something that is not too expensive."

The Duke was due to arrive at twelve o'clock, so Lucia and Georgie reached the High Street at ten thirty finding it virtually empty.

"Let's go to the gift shop first. We're sure to get something there," said Georgie.

Just as they reached the shop, Quaint Irene emerged. "Not going to see the Duke then Irene?" asked Lucia knowing what answer she'd get.

"The Duke! I've better things to do than go cow-towing to rich aristocracy. Anyway, I see you two darlings have given it a miss."

"Yes, we were wanting to do a bit of shopping while everyone was out of the way. You're coming to our little dinner on Christmas Eve I hope Irene?"

"Wouldn't miss it, my divine Lucia! I still have nightmares about you being swept away that time."

"Come along Lucia. We haven't time to chat. We should get these presents sorted," said Georgie as he hurried into the shop. They bought one or two things and then decided to try the jewellers along the street. As they began to walk on, a large car drew up ahead of them and a tall man got out.

"Georgie wait a minute!" Said Lucia pulling his arm "look isn't that the Duke?"

"Yes, it is I think. What's he doing in town? He's supposed to be arriving by train."

"Looks like he's up to his old tricks and avoiding the crowds. On his own as well I wonder where Mrs Simpson is?" Said Lucia hurrying over.

"She must be a duchess now. Sounds a bit Alice *in Wonderland*, don't you think?"

As they came towards him, he stopped and looked in the jeweller's shop window. "Everything's very nice," he observed as they drew level.

"Yes, aren't they?" said Lucia "and there's more to buy as things begin to improve after that horrible war."

"Oh I agree, much better. Do you live in the area?" He said with a smile.

"Yes, just up the road. I'm Lucia and this is Georgie Pillson, my husband."

"Pleased to meet you. People call me Eddie. I'm staying in the area with friends for Christmas. My wife was tired after our journey so while she had a rest, I thought I'd look round the town. I saw an article in *The Picture Post* a few weeks ago about Tilling and it looked really nice, such nice pictures too."

"Did you," said Georgie "we took the photos for that article and one of our friends wrote it."

"It was very good, the whole series has been good. I fully intend to visit Hexham Abbey since seeing it. I wonder if you have time to direct me to the church and I'd like to see that delightful house called *Mallard* or something."

"We can do better than that, "said Lucia looking very pleased. "We live at *Mallards*, you must come in for a little lunch."

"How kind, especially as you don't know me. I may be a burglar you know."

"I'm sure you're not. The church is just round here if you'd like to see it. We may catch the Padre, if we're lucky."

They spent a pleasant time looking round the church and wandering along some of the picturesque streets of the town, eventually ending up in the garden room at *Mallards* where Grosvenor provided a light lunch.

"Well, that was delightful. My wife will be so jealous when I tell her what a nice time I've had, but I really must be going. I've got to get to the railway station by twelve, so if you could point me in the right direction, I'll say good bye."

"Well," said Georgie as they watched him hurry down the road "would you believe it? He never told us he was the Duke, but he must be going to the station to see the town's people. He's going to be late it will be gone twelve before he gets there."

"I expect everyone will be still there though. How wonderful entertaining the Duke of Windsor for lunch. Wait till I tell Elizabeth she'll be so jealous."

\*\*\*

The next day, Lucia met Elizabeth on the High Street as usual.

"Any news?" Lucia asked.

"Yes, I managed to speak to the Duke and Duchess of Windsor yesterday Lucia, asked them if they'd had a good journey."

"Did you really Elizabeth? How exciting but I've got something even more exciting. Georgie and I weren't at the station because we were too busy having lunch with the Duke."

Elizabeth looked surprised. "Well Lucia, I am amazed, he must have rushed from the station to *Mallards*, although I thought I saw them drive out of town."

"No, we had lunch at about eleven thirty in the garden room before he went to the station. Such a nice man and very interested in the town after seeing the article in the magazine, he particularly wanted to visit the church. It must have been your photo that did it Elizabeth."

"Yes I'm sure it was, but it wasn't the Duke you had lunch with because he didn't arrive at the station until twelve o'clock."

"That's because he was with us." Lucia was a little worried because it was almost noon when he left *Mallards* and he couldn't have got to the station by twelve o'clock, Elizabeth must be mistaken about the time.

"I think it was about twelve when he walked to the station."

"Lucia, it's impossible! I saw him get off the train. He isn't Houdini. He couldn't have been leaving *Mallards* and getting off a train at the same time. I don't know who you had for lunch, but it wasn't the Duke."

"We can soon find out. I think I recognise his car coming down the street now."

As she spoke the Rolls Royce Lucia had seen yesterday was progressing down the street at a steady pace. People were waving as it passed and as it drew near Lucia could see the man from yesterday sitting in the front passenger seat. She also saw him speak to someone in the back of the car, as it drew level and stopped.

"Mrs Pillson" he called out, "I'm pleased I've caught you. The Duke did so want to meet you." At that moment, another man put his head out of the rear window of the car. Lucia could see that this was indeed the Duke and she could just see his wife sitting next to him in the back of the car.

"Mrs Pillson, my man has told me how kind you and your husband were to him yesterday and I wanted to thank you, even though it made him late arriving at the station. You must let us return the complement and visit us at Ardingly Park soon."

"Why it was no trouble. I'm delighted as it means I've been able to meet you at last."

"I'll send a car for you and your husband in a couple of days when we've settled in and you must come for lunch with us."

Before Lucia could thank him, he'd rolled up the window and they'd moved off down the street with people waving as they went.

"Now then Elizabeth," said Lucia. "It may not have been the Duke we entertained but it was the next best thing. I'll tell you all about our lunch with the Duke at our Christmas dinner. You and Benjy are coming I hope?"

"Of course, dear Lucia, wouldn't miss it for the world! I shall expect to see royalty there as you've become such good friend with them. Au reservoir."

\*\*\*

The day of Lucia and Georgie's special dinner party had arrived. Lucia had been busy all day getting everything ready and Diva had sent Janet round to help. The table was set with a little present wrapped beside each place. Lucia and Georgie would sit at the ends and down one side would be Mr and Mrs Wyse, Diva and Daisy and Robert Quantock. Across from them would be Elizabeth and Major Benjy, the Padre and Quaint Irene with her friend. This had worked out well as the Padre had called earlier to say that his wife wouldn't be able to attend as she had one of her migraines and needed to stay in bed for the day. Irene had also called to ask if she could bring her friend and Lucia had agreed. So, this made up the numbers to a round twelve. Lucia assumed that Irene's friend would be Tammy, who she'd heard was coming over from America again for the holidays.

At six o'clock, Susan and Mr Wyse arrived with Diva. They had dressed up for the occasion in furs and their showiest jewellery. Daisy and Robert had only to walk round from next door and they were the next to arrive. Grosvenor took their coats, announced them and showed them into the dining room where Georgie was busy handing out glasses of wine. He was wearing his red jacket with the white fur trimming and, as it was Christmas, he'd pinned a large reindeer brooch to the lapel. Elizabeth hurried in, without being announced, followed by Major Benjy.

"What a nice table," Elizabeth observed, checking to see who she was sitting next to. "You always do a good job of entertaining, Georgie and how very Christmassy you look."

"We do our best Elizabeth. Lucia will be down shortly."

At that moment, Grosvenor announced, "The Padre."

"How's your poor wife?" Asked Georgie as he came over. "I hope she isn't too bad."

"Och. It's a shame, she always gets these headaches if there is any excitement and the Duke and Duchess coming to Tilling has set them off, I'm afraid."

Lucia appeared in a loose flowing dress with a high neckline and long sleeves. "How very nice you look tonight," said Major Benjy, moving over to her "very nice indeed." He kissed her outstretched hand and accepted a glass of wine from Georgie "any whisky at all?" he asked.

"Benjy come over here and sit down." Elizabeth shouted to him.

They all found their places. "I hope Quaint Irene won't be late," Lucia said. At that moment Grosvenor announced, "Miss Irene Coles and friend." To everyone's surprise, Irene walked in not with Tammy but with Colin. They all knew him as he'd visited last summer and judged the art competition. Georgie nearly fell off his chair "Colin!" was all he was able to say.

"Yes, Colin and Tammy have come to stay for the academic break but poor Tammy is suffering from exhaustion after the flight so she's too tired to come tonight."

Colin walked round to Georgie and gave him a hug. "I've been so looking forward to seeing you again Georgie," he said.

"Come and sit with me," was all Georgie could manage to say as he got his breath back. "Elizabeth move up a space."

Despite Elizabeth's grumbling, the evening went well. Lucia gave everyone a full report on the luncheon visit the day before with the Duke and Duchess.

"Such a nice couple and she is so sophisticated for an American. Oh sorry Colin, no offence meant. We had salmon, how they came by it I don't know, I suppose if you're royalty it's no problem."

Irene was heard to mutter, "Bloody wealthy aristocrats can get anything."

When they'd finished eating, Janet came round with more wine and whisky for Mr Wyse and Major Benjy.

"Just leave the bottle," he whispered as she moved away.

"I just wanted to say a few words," Lucia said tapping her spoon on a glass. "At this time of year, I always think back to that terrible ordeal that Elizabeth and I went through when the floods swept us out to sea. Elizabeth was brave throughout and together we got through it and returned to our beloved Tilling." Elizabeth smiled round acknowledging the Padre's, "Well done both of you, thank the Lord."

"So, another year is nearly over. We have survived a terrible war and we all now hope that 1948 will be a good year."

Lucia continued. "So, raise your glasses to a bright and peaceful future."

**The End**

Printed in Great Britain
by Amazon